The Doctor of Desire

BOOKS BY ALLEN WHEELIS

The Doctor of Desire

a novel by

ALLEN

WHEELIS

W·W·Norton & Company

New York · London

Copyright © 1987 by Allen Wheelis

Published simultaneously in Canada by Penguin Books
Canada Ltd., 2801 John Street, Markham, Ontario L3R 1B4.
Printed in the United States of America.

The text of this book is composed in 11.5 / 14.5 Electra, with
display type set in Bernhard Modern Bold and Bernhard
Modern. Composition and manufacturing by
The Maple-Vail Book Manufacturing Group.
Book design by Margaret M. Wagner.

First Edition

Library of Congress Cataloging-in-Publication Data

Wheelis, Allen, 1915–
The doctor of desire.

I. Title.
PS3573.H44D6   1987   813'.54   86–21696

ISBN 0-393-02425-3

W. W. Norton & Company, Inc.
500 Fifth Avenue, New York, N. Y. 10110

W. W. Norton & Company Ltd.
37 Great Russell Street, London WC1B 3NU

1 2 3 4 5 6 7 8 9 0

Contents

MEDITATION

NOTE TO THE READER

THIS book probes the relation of despair to desire. It is of two parts. Those who would do their own thinking about living should start with the story—what happens, and to whom, and what happens next—and ignore all that follows.

Those who are weary of story, of the fictions that envelop us, who long for a glimpse of the real, should begin with the meditation, the way things are, the lechery, foolishness, insight, longing, all that improvised, shifting, inconsistent, broken-field running through life of which the story is made.

Those with a taste for both might observe the sequence indicated by numbers following the chapter titles on the contents page.

S T O R Y

A human being hardly ever thinks about
other people. He contemplates fantasms which
resemble them and which he has decked out
for his own purposes.

—IRIS MURDOCH

I   ∽◠◦

The Dream

HENRY MELVILLE struggles up from sleep as if from under water, lifting, stretching, comes awake sitting up, arm extended, reaching. The room reverberates with a cry. He was calling. Cora, his wife, sleeps undisturbed beneath his outstretched arm. The room is dark. Faint light from shuttered windows. Slowly the sense of tumult and loss gives way to the stillness around him, the whispering of wind in the cypress outside the window, and presently the deep warning of a foghorn. He lowers his arm, looks at the face beside him. Round cheek, dark curved eyebrow, short perky nose, curly hair. In this light she might still be twenty-four. He puts his hand on her thigh. She stirs slightly, moans. He feels more tenderly towards her sleeping. He removes his hand. She is not the one of whom he dreamed.

He goes into the dressing room, looks out to the bay. A river of fog drifts in under the Golden Gate Bridge, ponderously roils and twists beneath a waning moon, frays out near Alcatraz. The towers of the bridge stand up in a cloudless sky, the curved roadway is mostly clear, though now and then the shifting fog interrupts the string of golden lights. Few cars. He looks at the clock. Three-thirty.

He dresses, goes downstairs, leaves a note on the kitchen table. In the garage his old gray Buick stands beside Cora's trim new Audi, gun-metal blue. Vallejo to Divisadero, up the hill to Broadway, west to Lyon where he stops, looks out over the luminous fog, coiling and uncoiling. Eucalpytus trees in the Presidio stir slightly. He sees his own house, a mass of blackness except for the light he left on in the kitchen, thinks of the sleeping woman upstairs. She had her heart set on that house, watched it for years; now she has it. The fog glistens with ghostly whiteness under the crescent moon, and now from beneath that luminous surface, in darkness, comes the lowing of a ship, blinded beast feeling its way home.

Lyon to Washington to Laurel. He drives slowly, encounters no cars, looks about. Pacific Heights, Presidio Heights. Many of his patients live around here. Big houses. Sleeping people in large dark rooms. People who can afford psychoanalysis, who are in a position, therefore, to realize that they need it. He stops at Clay and Locust. An unmarked car cruises slowly, its spotlight probing the dark houses. This would be the moonlighting police officer looking after those clients who have engaged his special protection. For a long moment the spotlight falls on him, moves on. The car will circle around, check on him again. He starts home again, but at Broderick turns right to Sutter, pulls into his parking place at the Psychoanalytic Institute. He looks about before opening the door. The parking lot is in deep shadow, his office a block away. Not a safe place to be walking. Then it occurs to him—he must be distracted—at this hour he can leave his car anywhere. He drives on Sutter past Mt. Zion Hospital where, twice weekly, he teaches psychiatric residents. An ambulance, lights flashing, appears behind him, turns into the emergency entrance. At Scott he turns left, stops in front of his office. An old Victorian house, pre-earthquake; he has the front half. He lets himself in. Total darkness. Waiting room to the left. Proceeds straight ahead, up the circular stairs. His left hand trails the curved mahogany railing, reminds him of his dream. Another key—he knows it by touch—admits him to his office. He closes the door, sits at his desk. His fingers come down precisely on fountain pen, letter-opener, magnifying glass, scissors, paper clips. After a while he stands, goes to the wall of books, touches the spines. He is looking for something. Why doesn't he turn on the light? It wouldn't help. It isn't here. He lives in this room, knows what's here . . . and where.

In darkness he lies on the couch. A faint light comes through the gauze curtains. Again the falling two-tones of the foghorn, again the lowing of the blinded ship. He sees the luminous sky above, the necklace of golden lights, sinks down through the fog to the dark water where the unseeing ships move slowly, warily. He hears a car on Sutter Street, follows the sound as it passes Scott, grows faint, disappears around Steiner. Now a deep silence. He wants to sleep. Perhaps he will dream again. But something is stirring, he lies wakeful. Gradually the sounds of traffic begin, the room becomes light.

He goes to the bathroom, washes his face, looks in the mirror. He is a tall man, gaunt, hollow of frame, slightly stooped. His dark hair is thinning; when he combs it wet, large streaks of scalp glisten through. He is fifty-three years old. He reenters his office, sits in the chair behind the couch.

High ceilings, two pairs of French doors opening onto balconies. A beautiful room. Large, light, elegant. Polished teak floors, antique Caucasian rugs. A Klee drawing, *Man on a Tightrope*. Two walls of books, the multicolored spines a clamor of contending voices and visions, confined to order by solid walnut shelves. And clocks, clocks everywhere, of an accuracy so far exceeding his need as to become a celebration of time, the commodity he sells; he could no more do without clocks than a greengrocer his scales. A north wall entirely of glass. Light filigree curtains billowing in and out with the wind, he sees out but no one sees in. The room fills up, floor to ceiling, like a pool, with a diffuse gray light.

It is a room of listening, of longing. No action takes place here, only reflection and desire, and—he fingers his thinning hair—the inexorable passing of time. In the beginning was the word, in the middle was the word, and now, nearing the end, is still the word. When, if ever, will come the deed? The clocks measure out the listening into fifty-minute hours, the longing is continuous, flows on forever.

He has begun to have a recurring dream. A dark-haired woman, beckoning. She walks away. Turns, looks back, her head tilted as if asking why he does not join her. And he wants to. Desperately. He reaches out his arm, leans toward her, yearns toward her. But is mired, heavy-footed, while she glides lightly on. Again she turns, her expression quizzical, enigmatic, perhaps sad. She is entering a wood. The distance between them grows. Her dress glimmers. He struggles after, loses her in the darkness.

Sometimes she is disappearing down a stairway, looking back, delicate fingers lightly touching the dark curved handrail. This morning he almost reached her, brushed her fingertips. Her garments are light-colored, long and flowing. Her face is familiar, yet he does not know her. One such dream is interpreted and dismissed, but . . . every night. Surely this is a portent. The world is unchanged, something must be happening to him. He is getting old. He smells his death on the wind. When he wakes in the night he can smell it, faintly, on his own breath. But I'm not through yet, he thinks. I'm not all that old. I can run three miles in twenty-seven minutes. I have still a powerful serve. I'm good for one more big push. What shall it be?

II ∿∘

Dark Pools

SHE was a musician, she said, a pianist, had just moved to San Francisco. Her name was Lori Savella. Slight accent. From Venice, she said. The voice on the phone was dark and musical. The young woman who, a few days later, appeared in Dr. Melville's office was somewhat awkward in movement, intensely anxious, isolated, unable, she said, to make or keep a close attachment. She was both shy and arrogant, afraid to love because of its closeness to submission, drove men away in the very process of trying to indicate interest and availability.

She was a tall, slender girl, athletic, broad-shouldered, flat-chested, but with two features of remarkable softness and sensuality: large blue eyes, which sometimes deepened to violet, with curving lashes and darkly curving brows; and thick glistening chestnut hair with glints of red in a silken fall, parting at the line of her shoulders, currents shifting and interweaving with the movements

of her head, running now forward, now back, braiding
and purling like water over rocks, reminding Dr. Melville of that painting of Klimt's, *Wasserschlangen*, naked
bodies in flowing water, hair streaming backward in dark
transience. Sometimes she wore tight-fitting jeans, and
Dr. Melville—ever the sharp observer—noted that her
thighs did not come together at the top but showed some
space between; and, observing that transverse line of crotch,
himself unobserved behind the couch, he could not help
thinking of that fullness of genital parts which would make
for such space.

HER analysis gets off to a slow start, proceeds at a glacial pace. Long silences. Immense moraines of stasis.
Relates the external events of her life, sometimes an
impenetrable dream, nothing of feeling or passion. She
is a headliner, gives the captions, withholds the stories.
"I went to a party last night, met an interesting man."
Period. That's it. Whose party, Dr. Melville would want
to know, where, how many people, what were you wearing, how did you feel, what did the guy look like, how
tall, what's his name, what did he say, how did he look
at you, did he turn you on, what did you say, did you
blush, did you stammer, did you make a date. Nothing
of that. Just silence. Then another headline. Dr. Melville points out her guardedness; she agrees, wants to loosen
up, but can't, is far removed from feelings, does not know
how to get in touch with them, nor even to try. Free-
associate, he tells her. Nothing comes to mind, she says,
but these dull things, it's just resistance even to say them.

Why are you silent? he asks. She doesn't know, nothing in her mind. You are resisting, he tells her; there's always something in mind. It is not possible to be conscious without being conscious *of something*. What is it? She doesn't know, her mind is blank, she feels discouraged. He points out the silent areas, realms of necessary and ubiquitous experience, to some degree unavoidably conscious, which she never mentions: her body, its needs and functions, its itches and urgencies, gurgles and growls; her fantasies, vain or vulgar or sexual, grandiose or masochistic; her feelings about him, anger, love, fear.

"You are bored with me," she says softly. "It's all true what you say. You could not avoid being bored. You must regret having taken me as a patient. I'm afraid you're going to tell me that it's not working, that analysis is not suitable for me, that you will refer me to someone for psychotherapy."

One day she begins the hour with a dream. No associations. Silence. From the street the sound of a truck, a heavy turning around, the grinding of gears, voices of workmen. She seems to listen, says nothing. Presently the throbbing of a jackhammer which, after a few hesitations, settles down to a steady racket which then continues with but momentary interruptions, obliterating all other sounds. Impossible to talk. Must be a relief to her, Dr. Melville thinks, to have reality itself sanction her resistance. He gets up from his chair behind the couch, picks up the ottoman on which his feet had rested, places it by the couch. He sits now beside her head, leans forward, elbows on his knees. Before him at close range the expanse of her supine body. "It's hard to talk," he says, "but let's do the best we can. You talk a little louder and I'll listen a little harder. Let's try."

A few inches away her breast rises and falls with her breathing; at the edge of his vision a flush rises in her face; her hands are folded over her pubis, the long delicate fingers quiver slightly. She begins to talk, produces associations to the dream. He asks a question, associations come more freely, including two bits of relevant day residue, then an essential clue. The latent meaning is disclosed, the dream interpreted. She nods, it makes sense. At the end of the hour, as he opens the door for her, the jackhammer is still throbbing. "We did all right anyway," he says, and she smiles.

The next day she begins the hour, as usual, with silence, then takes a deep breath. "The main thing to talk about," she says, "is yesterday's hour, because I've been thinking about it ever since. I don't want ever to forget it. Because if I get stuck again, and I suppose I will, I'll need to remember it, and what it means, and then remind myself it's still true. That you would sit on that stool, that you would *lean over* to hear me . . . take me that seriously. I felt accepted. That's something new. I've never felt that before. It meant a lot, it makes a difference in the way I feel about myself. Many more things might be possible if I could hold on to that."

ANOTHER day, a few minutes after the end of her hour, Dr. Melville left his office. Dense, swirling fog. Across the street was Lori, still sitting in her car. He waved, she lifted her hand, he went on. Halfway down the block he turned; she had not moved. Strange. He walked back, crossed the street. "Is anything wrong?"

"My battery is dead. . . . I left my lights on."

"Have you called?" There was a pay-phone on the sidewalk.

She smiled ruefully. "I haven't any money."

He reached in his pocket, changed his mind. "Wait. Maybe I can help." He was back in a few minutes in his own car, bringing it up against hers. "Now . . . if you will release the hood." She got out,watched as he affixed the cables. "Now . . ." He straightened up, they were standing very close. Her eyes, in the gray mist, were midnight blue, expectant, trusting. She didn't move. Beside them his old heavy Buick, nose-to-nose with her slender, delicate BMW, both unbuttoned, exposed to each other, their intimate machinery linked together, his energy flowing into her—did she feel any of this? "Try it now," he said thickly. The motor started instantly, she smiled her thanks; he uncoupled them, closed the hood. She waved, drove away.

THE buzzer sounds, announcing a patient. That would be Charles Morgan, blocked and irascible writer. Dr. Melville presses the door release. A minute later some-one else arrives. Two patients claiming the same hour? Dr. Melville opens the door of his office, listens. Voices from below. He goes down. In the waiting room Charles Morgan and Lori Savella. Miss Savella is on her feet instantly, moving to mount the stairway.

"Miss Savella, you . . ." Dr. Melville glances at Charles

Morgan, back at the young woman. "Miss Savella," he says gently, "I'm afraid you've made a mistake. You've come at the wrong time." She seems not to understand, is waiting for him to stand aside that she may start up the stairs. "Your appointment is at two-thirty. Don't you remember?"

"Yes?" she says uncertainly.

"It's only one-thirty now."

"Oh!"

She is confused, stunned, as if she were being rejected altogether. Does she not realize it is but an hour's delay?

Charles is on his feet, touches her arm. "Please! Allow me . . . I'm in no hurry. Take my hour. I'd be so happy . . ."

She glances at him, nods in a dazed manner, still uncertain.

Dr. Melville looks at her questioningly, then turns to Charles Morgan, his expression becoming sardonic. "Miss Savella thanks you; I thank you. But we'd better stick to the schedule. Come in, please, Mr. Morgan. . . . I'll see you in one hour, Miss Savella. You are welcome to wait here if you wish."

In the office Mr. Morgan lies on the couch, groans. "Oh God! I can't stand it. How do you get to be a psychoanalyst? I want to apply. Imagine! To be alone with her for an hour—hour after hour, day after day—to hear her secrets, her desires. You even get paid for it! I'd do it for free. I'd pay her! I'm burning with envy. What a beautiful woman! I can't bear it. Why does God do this to me?"

DAY after day the Venetian lies on the couch. Motionless. From behind her Dr. Melville regards the slim extended body. Soft chestnut hair in lustrous waves. His hand trembles with contained touching. Small breasts, flat belly, smooth bulge of mons veneris. Legs straight and still.

She talks in a low voice, hesitantly; does not seize her experience, cannot pick it up firmly, turn it around, take it apart; approaches it diffidently, with silences, uncertainties, ambivalence. Nothing is clear, she is lost, confused, feels hopeless, dreams he will save her.

Day after day. For fifty minutes. And, as each session ends, Dr. Melville says, his voice like a caress, "We must stop now."

She sits up, puts her feet on the floor, reaches for her purse. At the same moment the two of them stand. She waits as he goes before her, opens the door. He stands aside, turns, watches. As she approaches, the long curved lashes are lifted, she looks at him. This is the moment. Their eyes meet. She smiles. That look! That look! What does it mean? Vulnerable, helpless, timidly desiring, enticing, dangerous . . . maddening! Dr. Melville reels, dives through those widened pupils, swoons, down, down, in fathomless depths, drowns—while his face registers no more than the slight smile and detached kindness allowable to a psychoanalyst.

"Good-by."

"Good-by."

The lashes are lowered. She passes. He moves slightly as if to follow. She starts down the stairs. Before she disappears from view she glances back, one last time, and once more he is falling into her dark waters. Then she is gone. His heart swells with pain, bursts. He staggers back into his office. He is dying.

SHE has forgotten her coat! And he too! It lies across the chair where he laid it. So taken up were they with looking into each other's eyes . . . He snatches it up, runs after her, down the stairs, out the front door; sees the silver BMW disappear around the corner of Pine Street. He returns to his office. The coat is leather, bitter chocolate, dark silk lining. Pleated in back, flared skirt, no belt, unusually long yet very light. The leather is supple and thin, flows and falls like fabric. Italian. He examines the pockets. A symphony ticket, one stub—did she go alone? A folded linen handkerchief, edged with lace. A tortoise shell comb. He drapes the coat over his legs, moves his hands over the surface. Closes his eyes, the better to take in the texture. He caresses the coat. It feels like skin, a woman's belly. He sniffs the lining, a faint perfume; he inhales deeply, wanting to smell her body, her very *self*. He covers his head completely, is in darkness, moans slightly, puts his arms around the woman who, absent, still somehow inhabits this coat, draws her to him, holds her tightly.

IN warm weather Lori often wears a sleeveless belted tunic of mulberry or mauve or lemon, with white tapered slacks of cotton or linen and white canvas espadrilles without socks. Some of these tunics have low sweeping necklines which expose the upper part of her chest, the beginning swell of breasts. She is a sun-worshipper and her skin in summer is a dark tan. She lives in a house of two flats of which she has the upper; both tenants have access to a roof garden, and it is there on clear days she lies on a deck chair in a bikini. The other tenant, a bachelor, talks to her whenever he can, invites her for a drink or to dinner. Dr. Melville is jealous, envious, longs for that man's freedom to climb the stairs to that roof, to discover her there almost naked, to engage her in conversation; for nothing prevents that fortunate man from going as far with her as he can. Though of course, as Dr. Melville knows, such envy would but exchange one set of barriers for another: To Dr. Melville she is accessible, defenseless, the obstacle within him, the analytic situation; yet her fellow tenant, with no such constraint, finds her equally unreachable, the stops in her being equally final. He never gets to first base.

Sometimes on Mondays after a hot weekend she enters Dr. Melville's office with newly deepened color, a dusky rose, glowing as if the sun, so recently playing over her skin, still burned in its pores. The slim ankles gleam darkly between the white pants and the white canvas shoes. The fine hair of her arms, bleached, has become visible. The darkness of this still slightly inflamed skin seems to make it more passionate, more receptive of impulse, more knowing of sin. From the slender neck this darkness extends down over bony clavicles, down, down, disappearing maddeningly under the neckline of the tunic. Are the breasts themselves so brown? Does she take off her bra to the sun? Dr. Melville envies that sun to whom she so opens and exposes herself—as, in fact, in a way, she does also to him—but who is free of those constraints which hold Dr. Melville in check, that sun whose rays reach out and touch her, caress her so intimately, so exactly as would Dr. Melville's restless empty hands.

LORI is weeping, but her wet, unlined face is radiant. An hour ago she had walked stiffly into this room, lay on the couch, crumpled up, cold, nothing to say, no feeling, staring, mute. What do you feel? Dr. Melville asked. What's on your mind? Did you dream last night? What happened after you left here yesterday? Whom have you seen? What did you eat? Did someone telephone you? On and on, without much response, an evasive word now and then, turning more and more away, inward, face to the wall, on and on, persisting, until finally he breaks through to some warded-off feeling, and now the hour is over, he is exhausted, but the sleepwalker is awake. He stands, goes before her to the door. As she starts to pass he touches her arm.

"Sometimes," he says, "on a day like this, when your voice is small and distant, when feelings are far away, when all is confusion and loss, it seems to me that I am walking on a shore in a gray mist, looking for you." She trembles. He has never spoken to her in the doorway. "And I call, 'Lori! Lori!' But you don't answer and I can't find you. I keep looking and calling, 'Lori! Lori!' and finally, very faintly, I hear your voice. I look about, here and there, and then I see you—far out in the icy water." She moves. His fingers tighten on her arm. "I swim to you. You float inertly, you are almost frozen, only your eyes move. The eyes say, 'Help me.' I put my arm around you, hold your face above water, and take you to shore. And rub your body, cover you with blankets, and after a while you begin to smile and cry, to be happy, to be sad, to dance . . ." Still in the doorway, halfway between the safe unreality of the couch and the dangerous world outside, she is shaking, her expression pleading. "And I think: I hope she watches what I do, that it become part of her, that some day when she may find herself again in that icy water, and I am not there, she will *remember*—and, alone, will swim for shore."

THE last hour before a three-week interruption.

"I beg your pardon?" Dr. Melville says.

"I was mumbling," Lori says, ". . . because it's . . . hard to say."

"And what were you mumbling?"

"That I will miss you."

"And why is it so hard to tell me that?" His voice is soft and encouraging.

"I don't know. Dependence, I guess. . . . I'm so afraid of . . . leaning on you."

"Does missing someone have to imply leaning?"

"Perhaps."

"Would it be equally hard," he asks gently, "for you to say . . ." he pauses, ". . . 'I love you'?"

She is silent for a full minute. "That would be quite impossible!"

How devious I am, he thinks ruefully. My question

would have her believe I am measuring a degree of diffi-
culty, but I'm not measuring anything, am not asking a
question at all. I want to say, "I love you"; and that pause,
separating the declaration from the perfunctorily framing
question, leaves it on its own. I want her to hear it that
way, yet to believe it to be but her fantasy that it might
have been so meant, encouraging her thereby to such
sentiments of her own.

Ah, well, psychoanalysts, too, need to be loved.

ORDINARILY Dr. Melville does not shake hands with
those patients whom he sees several times weekly; but on
this occasion, at the door, since they will not meet for a
while, he extends his hand and experiences once more—
though now with far greater intensity—something of their
first clasp of hands. Her hand, the hand of a pianist, strong,
slender, with long fingers, takes his hand with a firmness
equal to that of his own. And with something more,
something peculiarly her own, a locked-in quality as if
this contact, now made, will not end. Her whole arm is
tense, he feels a faint quiver. She is not inclined to *shake*
his hand, is intent on *holding* it—a grip that means
something, you could lift a person with such a hold—
and as they stand there in the doorway her eyes lock on
his with an intensity he finds electrifying. The two of
them are linked by a double bond, united identically by
flesh and gaze, a closed circuit through which flows, circles, round and round between them, a current of intense
and intensely reciprocated feeling. He speaks a few words
of good-by and good wishes, and she replies, but neither

of them hears or attends to the words, there is no wavering of that locked gaze.

And now, their hands still in tight clasp, Dr. Melville feels an increase in that tremor of arm, a certain awkwardness of tense readiness in her slightly elevated shoulder, her entire body, and knows instantly what it means. She is afraid of detaining him, of holding him too long, of being possessive, and so perhaps of imposing or of offending, yet will not, or cannot, herself abandon the contact, cannot initiate that dreaded letting go; so the quiver represents her heightened alertness to a sign from him.

Dr. Melville wants to live forever in the current of passion that envelops them, circles through them, wants to take her shoulder with his left hand, draw her close. The words stop, the lips are still, the moment extends itself, reaches the far limit of convention, of propriety, stretches that limit thin; it is up to him, his responsibility, not hers.

He relaxes his grip, and instantly she lets go, withdraws her hand. She smiles, nods, turns, starts down the stairs, looks back and up, and once more that locked gaze, that falling into dark waters, and then she is gone.

I I I ⁓⌒。

R o m a n c e

"MISS SAVELLA. Come in."

One dark glance as she enters. Smoldering face. Dr. Melville helps her off with her coat. She blushes, goes quickly to the couch, lies flat on her back, her legs straight, close together, arms at her sides. Dr. Melville sinks back into his soft leather chair, extends his crossed legs on the ottoman, looks out the window, waits.

Silence. Minutes pass.

"What are you thinking?"

"Nothing."

"What do you feel?"

"Nothing. My feelings seem to be hidden away. Locked up. I can't get at them."

"What are you aware of?"

"I don't know. Nothing."

"It is hardly possible to be conscious," Dr. Melville explains carefully, as he has so often in the past, "without being conscious *of* something. You are aware of things, but are discounting them, dismissing them. Perhaps they seem too trivial, perhaps too personal, maybe embarrassing, even offensive. Try not to allow any such normative standard . . ." even as he says it he feels distaste for the jargon phrase ". . . to act as a censorship."

Silence. Minutes pass.

"What have you been aware of during this silence?"

"Nothing. My mind is blank."

"That is not possible. You are resisting. Perhaps without knowing it. How do I know? Because of the silent areas." How many times, he thinks wearily, have I said all this. "Realms of experience that never get mentioned, but which from time to time must necessarily enter your awareness. *Must* because they are part of being human, of being conscious. For everybody. For example, the vulgar, the obscene. You never use a dirty word, never a spiteful thought or fantasy. Everything you've said, over all these months, has been courteous, decorous. 'All the news that's fit to print.' Could all have been on the front page of the *Times*. Another silent area is that of your reactions to me. You must have thoughts and feelings about the one who listens. It's inevitable. Yet another such area is your body and its sensations. You never report an itch or a cramp or the rumblings in your gut, or a full bladder. These are but a few of many silent areas. Try to bring some of these things into verbalization."

Silence. Minutes pass.

"What are you thinking?"

"Nothing."

"What have you been aware of during these past few minutes?"

"I don't know. It's hard. I've been aware that I have to think of something, that if I don't I will fail. I'm not a good patient. You must be bored with me. I'm afraid you will say I can't be analyzed. I'm terrified you will send me away."

"So! You *are* aware of something. You are afraid of rejection. Tell me more about that. What comes to mind?"

Silence. Minutes pass.

"What are you thinking?"

"I'm trying to bring something to mind . . . but can't think of anything."

"Don't think about failing. I know you are trying. Your effort must be taking place within an unnoticed frame. Like the frame of a picture. You are attending only to that part of the field of consciousness which lies within that frame and are asking yourself, what do I see? And you see nothing. The field is blank. But outside that frame are all those things you don't want to talk about. 'They don't count,' your resistance says, 'keep quiet about them.' You are aware of them, but peripherally. You don't have to look directly at them in order to see them; but since these things lie outside the frame within which you are trying to free associate you don't attend to them, don't even feel any conflict about not saying them. They are excluded in principle, by the frame. What you must do is expand the frame of free association until it becomes co-extensive with the field of awareness. Then you will find that it is truly not possible to be conscious and yet not be conscious *of* something."

Silence. Minutes pass.

"What are you thinking?"

"Nothing."

"What do you feel?"

"Nothing. My feelings are far away. They are locked up in a closet. I can't get at them."

"Open the door of that closet."

"It's locked. I have no key."

"Let's look for that key. Let's start off with your body. Are you aware of any sensations from your body?"

"My body feels numb."

"Are you cold?"

"No, just numb."

"Any sensations from your head?"

"No."

"From your chest?"

"No."

"From your belly?"

"No."

"From your genitals?"

Long silence. "Yes."

"Are you excited?"

"No."

"What do you feel?"

"Just an intense awareness. A kind of vividness. But this sensation doesn't seem to be between my legs. It's as though my genitals were detached, were out there in the air somewhere. . . . Drifting away." Now I don't feel it any more."

"What do you feel now?"

"My body seems numb."

"Do you feel anything in your legs?"

"My legs are numb."

"Why do you lie so still?"

"I don't know."

"Are you trying to lie still? I mean, are you making an effort not to move?"

"No."

"You must be. You just don't know it. Because you lie absolutely still. Motionless. You are *holding* yourself still. No one can be that still except by effort. It's defensive. It's one of the ways you keep feelings locked up in that closet. Emotions begin in the body. By lying on the couch as if in a coffin, you freeze feelings at the source."

"I know you're right."

"Are you afraid to move?"

"I don't know."

"Why don't you try?"

Minutes pass. "I *am* afraid."

Long silence.

"What are you thinking?"

"If you would tell me what to move . . . maybe I could do it."

"Try lifting one of your legs."

Long silence. "Which one?"

"The right one."

Presently the right leg begins to levitate. So slowly that for a while Dr. Melville is not sure there is any movement at all. But yes, now the foot is clear of the couch. The entire extremity, rigid, cantilevered from her hips, is suspended an inch or so above the couch. The movement is imperceptible, the effort to see it is hypnotic. She is not waking from the dead, Dr. Melville thinks, she is showing me the kind of sepulchral movement that might still be possible in the grave. How to move without cracking the body armor, that's what it is. Could be the title of a paper. Anything more rapid might disturb the defenses. The leg is now at about forty-five degrees. The skirt slips, comes half way down the silken thigh. A slight tremor runs along the leg; the movement stops. All is frozen. A slight jerk of her right hand, as if to replace the skirt. Instantly aborted. The hand is again inert. Presently the tomblike movement is resumed. The leg continues its glacial upward ambit. How utterly remarkable! The leg doesn't bend at the knee, moves as a single member. Now the skirt slips the rest of the way, lies about her hips. Now the leg is vertical. Movement stops. The assigned task is complete. The silence has become intense, so highly charged a chance spark might cause an explosion. Neither of them moves a muscle, neither seems even to breathe. Dr. Melville looks at the leg. Only his eyes move, sweeping up and down the exhibited member. He is spellbound. His consulting room has become a museum. The statue of Aphrodite has stirred slightly in her marmoreal sleep, is offering him a private showing, a different view of her immortal charms.

Oh God! he thinks. A frozen goddess asking to be thawed, desperate for the warmth of my body to drive away that catatonic rigor in hers. And I am not allowed! Am forbidden to touch!

"Our time is up," he says gently.

She does not move immediately, but sighs deeply, then lowers her leg.

ANOTHER day. Miss Savella lies still and silent on the couch.

"What are you thinking?"

"Nothing."

"What are you aware of?"

"My coat."

"What about your coat?" .

"I don't know. . . . Nothing."

"A special coat?"

"The brown leather."

"And what about it?"

"I don't know. . . . Nothing."

Silence. "What comes to mind?"

"I left it here once. Forgot it."

"Yes?"

"Nothing . . . No reason to remember that."

"Associate. Imagine it just as it happened. You are lying on the couch, your coat lies on the chair. The hour ends. You leave, forgetting your coat."

"It occurs to me . . . I wonder . . . what happened to the coat after I left?"

"What do you think?"

"I don't know. Nothing. The next day it was . . . still . . . on the chair."

" 'Still' or 'again'?"

"Oh! I don't know. This is tiresome."

"Is not the issue what I did with the coat after you left?"

"I don't know. I can't imagine why, or how it could matter. Or to whom."

"Perhaps you wonder: Did I touch it? Did I hold it? Did I enter its pockets? Explore its secret places? Or perhaps . . . what happened to it overnight?"

"This is so silly. . . . It makes me uncomfortable."

Long silence.

"By the way," Dr. Melville said, "why didn't you wear the coat today?"

"I did."

"Where is it?"

"In the waiting room."

"That's a first, isn't it?"

"Yes."

"Always you've worn it in here?"

"Yes."

"And why not today?"

"So you would not have to help me out of it."

"Does that bother you?"

"It's an imposition."

"Imposition? How so?"

"It must be a bother for you. To help me out of my coat, day after day, to fold it, put it on a chair."

"No bother at all. I've hardly noticed. It bothers *you*. You are projecting your reaction onto me."

"I think you're right."

"In what way does it bother you?"

"I don't know."

"What comes to mind?"

"When you take it off you're so close. You stand behind me. . . . Now I feel nervous, just talking about it."

"Are you afraid I will touch you?"

"I don't know."

"Do you *want* me to touch you?"

"No. Well . . . I'm not sure."

"You don't say anything about my helping you *on* with your coat before you leave. Yet I do that too. Just as often. Why does your nervousness focus only on my taking it off?"

"I don't know."

"Could it be that this simple courtesy stands in your mind as symbolic of a more radical uncovering? That my helping you out of your coat presents itself to your imagination as but the first act of undressing you altogether?"

Silence.

"What do you feel?"

"My face is hot. I think you are right."

"So, we can reconstruct why that coat now hangs in the waiting room. You have sexual desires toward me. These desires generate fantasies. The fantasies cause anxiety because the incest barrier forbids such feelings for a father, and I am like a father. So the fantasies are warded off, repressed. But when I come up to you from behind, stand close to you, almost touch you, and take off your coat—this is very like your hidden wish that I make love to you. As this wish approaches consciousness you feel anxiety. The anxiety prompts you to leave your coat outside. You then rationalize your act with the idea of sparing me the bother of assisting you."

"I know you're right."

"These warded-off fantasies should be examined. Try now to bring them into full consciousness."

"I don't think I can. I don't think I dare."

"We know already that you have such desires. Why then should talking about them seem so dangerous?"

"It would make them more real. Closer to being acted upon."

"The basic faith of psychoanalysis is that it is better to know than not to know, that we are in better control of our desires if we know what they are."

"I'm afraid to believe that. It seems just *knowing* what I want to do becomes the start of trying to do it. And *talking* about it is then the *second* step. If it's wrong to do it, I'd better not get started . . . or even know I want it."

"That is, certainly, the way you feel. That's the resistance. It's the sign on that closet door where your feelings are locked up. 'Keep out!' But it is not a principle you should honor. Our passions reach out variously toward many things. How can we decide what to permit, what to forbid, unless we are free, in the laboratory of thought, to examine what we desire? To evaluate, to consider the likely consequences? Be less frightened of your desires. Put more trust in the laboratory of thought."

Silence.

"What are you thinking?"

"I'm thinking that tomorrow I will want to wear my coat in here. But that will mean I *want* you to take it off. And that will mean that . . . I feel very hot. I'm frightened."

WHEN she had gone—disappeared down the stairway with that last look back and up, that slight smile, that secret and mysterious message—yearning rose up in Dr. Melville with a constricting pain. He felt himself choking. It seemed to originate at some depth, to press against a containment, to break through suddenly, welling up in a dark flood. He wanted to talk to her, to stroke her hair, hold her hand, wanted to convince her of her worth, to persuade her by his devotion that her fear of inadequacy and of rejection were neurotic fictions, that what she so desperately sought was right at hand, spread out before her eyes.

The longing kept welling up, overflowing. His role was a straitjacket. The space behind the couch was closing in, he couldn't move, couldn't breathe. How break out of it? How find his way to her? Someday, somehow, it must be possible. It *has* to be.

But she was twice barred to him: In the second instance because Cora, his wife, stood in the way. Cora, who noticed everything, who did not ask questions, did not depend for information on his words, no more than a hawk would wait for reports of mice. She observed, she inferred—asked questions only for street addresses and telephone numbers. After Cora was dead—*then* it might be possible. But she was hardly fading away. She wasn't going to die. It was he who would die first! He felt a sinking, found himself in a swamp, realized suddenly how much he had been sustained by the hope—the illusion!—that some day he would again be free for the fumbling encounter, the desperate ignorance, of love. How could he live were he to know that this could never happen?

As if to confirm that it would not, he felt a pain in his upper abdomen. A gnawing pain. The same pain, come to think of it, as yesterday, as of rather often recently. He had been thinking of it vaguely as gallbladder. Or perhaps ulcer. But this is the kind of pain with which pancreatic cancer announces itself. Sooner or later it will happen. That or something like that will make itself known by some such pain as this. So what then? What if next week he should know for sure? Lori's face was still before him, her body, the dark flood still surging up. It must still, even so, be possible. Some way. How?

"I have to tell you something difficult," he would say to her. "This will be painful for you, but there's nothing for it. It has to be faced. I am not well, will not live long. So far I have not much pain, will continue to work—so long as I can. That's the good thing, that we have time, a matter of months perhaps. We must work through what this means to you, so you will not experience it as another desertion. This is our task. We must do what we can." She will be mute with shock, will come to her next hour with swollen eyes. "I can't do it," she will say. "Not analytic work. It's impossible. I can't talk about myself, my little anxieties, my inhibitions." "I understand," he will say, "I was afraid of that." "But I can't stop seeing you either," she adds quickly. "What would help me most would be to sit up, to talk *with* you. You shouldn't have to *work* with me any more. You've done enough. Why don't I come now as a friend? The same hours as before . . ." What a cunning idea he has fathered in her mind, the only way he could see her personally without Cora knowing.

So four times a week, as before, she would arrive at his office, but would no longer lie on the couch. She would *sit* on the couch and he would sit beside her. He would talk about himself, would tell her many things. And his approaching death would enable her to talk more intimately and more freely. She would know herself to be important to him, would thereby overcome her inhibitions, her sense of inadequacy, and these meetings would acquire a special and deepening resonance. Nothing morbid. Often they would laugh. Would feel this time together as a great gift, given to few, one of life's rare jackpots. They would hold hands, would touch. Sometimes her head would rest against his shoulder. He would stroke that opulent glistening hair, that silken mystery of promise, of exotic scent. Between such dissimilar lovers would develop a perfect reciprocity. They would play together, would fit together, would interweave like the strains of a Schubert duet. A generation apart, yet terribly close. One departing life (C minor cello, present menace subdued by distant serenity) as one entered the fullness of life (brilliant violin passage in E flat major). The two in matching beat, in perfect time. Divided by nothing, no jealousy, no demands, no possessiveness. No future, just this dancing bountiful present, going on and on. He would give to her of his experience and wisdom, she had much to learn and a great eagerness; and she would give to him of her inexhaustible youth. Both would be enriched . . . and sometimes they would lie together on the couch.

I V

Lecture

A HALF circle of steeply rising tiers. The noon lecture, open to all departments and to the public. Dr. Melville sat in the front row chatting with the chairman, a bio- chemist, who would introduce him. The room was fill- ing rapidly, many of Dr. Melville's colleagues were present. Cora sat near the center. Lori Savella came in, took a seat near the front. Cora observed her closely. Lori saw Dr. Melville, blushed, averted her eyes. Cora's glance darted back and forth between them. A few minutes later Charles Morgan entered, sat in the back, spotted Miss Savella, came forward to join her. Before he could reach her a young woman with an armful of notebooks took the seat. Mr. Morgan scrambled for the nearest available place, two rows behind her and four in from the aisle. This maneuvering, also, Dr. Melville observed, had been taken in by Cora.

Now, at one minute before twelve, people were

crowding in through all doors: interns, residents, nurses, medical students, psychiatrists, social workers, psychologists. Two analytic candidates, analysands of Dr. Melville, entered together, sat in the back row. "You're pulling a full house," the chairman said. Dr. Melville felt a thrill of pleasure, also that edginess, that chalkiness of mouth which, he knew, would disappear as he began to talk. The paper was in his briefcase, but already he knew he would not read it. He was caught up in the exhilaration of performance, of showing himself, of wanting to be seen, touched, by so many eyes; but at the same time, embarrassed, rueful, at such a welling up of narcissism. The chairman went to the lectern, Dr. Melville's appointments and honors were enumerated, he came forward to a generous applause, the chairman fitted the microphone around his neck.

The student beside Lori spotted a friend, waved, gathered up her notebooks, moved away. Charles Morgan was instantly on his feet going for the aisle, squeezing by the surprised and obstructing knees, reaching Miss Savella in time to claim the seat. They exchanged a few words, she nodded, he sat beside her.

Dr. Melville began to talk about responsibility. A universal idea, he said, ubiquitous, confusing. One can say nothing more significant about a person than that he is responsible or that he is irresponsible. We all use these terms, they represent one of our most basic judgments. Yet the concept of responsibility is hardly mentioned in scientific literature. You'd think that psychiatrists and psychologists had not heard about it. In fact, they know it as well as anybody, and use it the same way as others.

When they speak nonprofessionally, that is. When they speak to their patients, or when they read papers at psychoanalytic meetings, they avoid it, use different words. Also more words. Usually a lot more. Conflict, ambivalence, distortion, undoing, et cetera. Why this discrepancy, this double standard? Because, he would suggest, the concept of responsibility falls across the border of psychology and morality, lies half in one realm, half in the other; so it is not possible to deal with it as a purely psychological issue. To deal with it at all is to get mixed up in the moral question, and this, as everybody knows, makes psychiatrists nervous. They would rather leave all that to the moralists. A fate that is shared, he suggests, by the concepts of freedom and of will which are closely related.

"So, let us talk about responsibility. And let us accept as a premise, on faith, that there *is* such a thing, that our subject is not an illusion; that is to say, that it makes sense to expect ourselves and others to be responsible. We part company at the start, therefore, with all who believe that human history was written in advance by invariant causal sequences, or in our genes, or in our stars. Any such who may be present are duly warned."

His nervousness was gone, he had left lectern and text, was beginning to walk about before the audience. It occurred to him, with a sort of remote sadness, that he loved to perform, to stand before a group, a multitude, to offer himself—his face, his body, his mind—as a focus for all those eyes, to begin to work that audience, to sound it out, first to sense and then to manipulate its mood, to capture its fickle attention, to begin to cast a spell, to charm, to seduce. It was like making love. In no other situation was he so alive, so engaged. I should have been an actor, he thought, or a musician or a dancer, should be doing something like this all the time. He had chosen the opposite extreme, lived behind a couch, could not be seen at all. He didn't talk, he listened. As far from performing as one could get. As a young man he had been most afraid of what he most wanted; and, as fear was stronger than desire, his vocation had been chosen by fear. Only now, he thinks, when it's too late, have I overcome the fear and come to know how much I enjoy showing off, being on stage.

In joint endeavors, he continued, responsibility is shared. Both, or all, are responsible. How this responsibility is to be apportioned, however, is not a matter of fact, but of choice. It cannot be discovered by examining the circumstances, it is a declaration of soul. Unilateral. Unchallengeable. An example chosen to illustrate this will necessarily be an example of failure; for the reason that in successful endeavors there is never any problem about responsibility: each participant is happy to accept as much responsibility as may be ascribed to him. Any example, therefore, will be one of failure. "Let's say an analysis which fails. A matter I know something about."

Miss Savella was caught up in rapt adoration; Mr. Morgan seemed removed, perhaps sardonic.

"Let us imagine, then, an analysis in trouble. Perhaps the analysand has stopped talking. Hours pass in silence. Eventually patience and money run out, the analysand quits. Analyst and analysand, let us suppose, are in agreement that the analysis has failed. The question is the responsibility for the failure. How it is to be formulated. Upon this the two participants likely will not agree. The analyst may say to himself, 'The patient had too much resistance. He—or she—was not analyzable. After all, I can't be expected to analyze if the patient won't talk.' Note that this formulation ascribes all responsibility to the patient; the analyst retains none. Or the analyst might say, 'Had I been more alert, more sensitive to early indications of resistance, more active in the interpretation of hidden negative transference, the impasse would not have developed.' This formulation claims all responsibility for the analyst. Intermediate formulations are possible; all the conceptual problems, however, may be encountered with but these two extreme ascriptions.

"The two formulations are logically equal. That is to say, each provides a comprehensive explanation of the event in question. Moreover, each may be demonstrably true. That is to say, each may be made to stand solidly upright on equally solid plinths of objective evidence. We may say, therefore, they are equally true."

As he got in the swing of it, he moved to and fro, felt his body grow lithe, sinuous. His breathing deepened, his voice gained resonance and authority. Without a pause he lifted the microphone from his neck, observing, as he did so, the people in the back rows. Everyone could hear; his unamplified voice filled the room. His slow pace was describing an ellipse within the available space, and when this ambit next brought him by the lectern he deposited the microphone. Unencumbered now by trailing wire, he felt an exhilarating lightness. His words had picked up the pace of his thought, his steps the rhythm of his words; and in the way in which, if rightly timed, the locked step of marching men can set a bridge in motion, so now he was hitting it just right, was conducting the responsive thought of this audience with an absolute baton. If he didn't push it too far, didn't stumble, he could do as he wished. He felt tremendous power, a kind of soaring. His body had become a phallus within this womblike space.

"They are not, however," he went on, "equal in their implications. For if one elects the first account, though he avoids responsibility for that particular failure, he is stuck with an explanation which offers no hope of avoiding such failure in the future. Whereas if one elects the second account, though he is burdened with responsibility for the present failure, he has in hand an explanation which can function as a tool, enabling him to avoid such failure in the future."

Mr. Morgan put his arm around Miss Savella, squeezed her shoulder, while she, spellbound, did not notice. Mr. Morgan gave his analyst a wicked grin.

Obviously the analysand, Dr. Melville went on, dealing with this same failure, may arrive at comparably counterposed explanations, one of which ascribes blame to the analyst and one of which claims blame for himself.

The important principle which emerges from such considerations is as follows: The larger the realm of experience for which one can claim and establish responsibility, the larger the realm of one's freedom. He would hope, therefore, that in the instance of a failed analysis he would elect the second explanation, claiming all of the responsibility, seeking thereby to locate variables within his control which would enable him to avoid failure in similar circumstances in the future.

"Do note, however, that it is not enough to *accept* responsibility, or to *claim* it, one must *establish* it. That is to say, one must locate variables within one's range of discretion and of action which could have changed the outcome. To claim responsibility in the absence of having found such variables is nothing but neurotic guilt. In its extreme it is masochism. All of us are familiar with the person who, whatever the mishap, instantly takes the blame, often without the foggiest notion of how he might have prevented it."

Lori was watching him with wide, adoring eyes, an unwavering gaze that pulled him like a magnet. She had lost her self-consciousness, her shyness, seemed rather to be hypnotized, melting into him. Charles's hand was slowly stroking her shoulder. Dr. Melville wrenched himself back to his subject.

"So, let me restate the principle. *The larger the realm of experience for which one can claim and establish responsibility, the larger the realm of one's freedom.*"

This principle, he went on, is equally true for all participants of a shared endeavor. Without ever thinking about it we assume that the total responsibility cannot exceed one hundred percent, that this responsibility, therefore, should be parceled out in equitable portions, like pieces of a pie. The assumption is fallacious. The total assumed responsibility, if there are two participants, may be two hundred percent. For three, three hundred. (And of course we are all too familiar with situations in which nobody accepts any responsibility.) The acceptance by one participant of full responsibility constitutes no reason why another participant should not also accept full responsibility. In such matters it is better that the participants do not agree, nor concern themselves with each other's view, but that each claim the whole responsibility.

"Therefore, when, in talking to a patient, I urge him to accept full responsibility for his depression, for his suffering, for his unhappy life, I am aiming for an increase in the scope of his freedom and his choice, but am in no way implying a reduction in the extent of my responsibility for the endeavor is which we are jointly engaged."

HE felt good about the talk. People crowded around him, a tone of exhilaration in their comments. They had been stimulated, sensed some mystery or magic in what he had said. He had cast a spell. As he stood there listening, responding, he was watching his two patients. Charles was speaking earnestly to Lori who seemed to hesitate. He was trying to persuade her, talk her into something.

V *~∘*

Aphrodite Unmoved

"GOOD evening, Mr. Morgan," the maître d' says, "Good evening, mademoiselle." He bows deeply, extends his right arm in spacious welcome. "I have a very nice table for you." He takes their coats, passes them to an assistant. "Right this way, please." He pulls out the chairs, assists them in being seated. "Will you be comfortable here?" He directs one assistant to alter a nearby curtain to obviate a possible draft, another to adjust the lighting a bit more perfectly. "Will you have a little drink before ordering?" Lori doesn't want anything. Charles urges her. She agrees, doesn't seem to care. Martinis are served. Presently, Henri, the maître d' is back. "Are we ready now to order?" His deference is more than respectful, it is struck with awe; he and his establishment, it would appear, are deeply honored by their presence.

Charles is annoyed. They are not really being treated as royalty, as Henri would have them think, but as pretenders to royalty, while Henri, aware of the pretense, chooses by virtue of his superior manners not to expose them. This is the ultimate revenge of the servant, Charles thinks: the obsequiousness, which ascribes to me the spurious status, manages also to imply that it is I who am claiming it, not he who, by his awed servility, is ascribing it. By accepting it I incur a guilt which will call for a larger tip. Meanwhile, the servant gets off scot-free; for, since the status is spurious, so too is his servility. The bowing and scraping is a charade; he can pocket the guilt-inflated tip with undiminished arrogance, the innocent beneficiary, as it were, of my vanity.

That arrogance is now plainly visible in Henri's handling of waiters and bus boys. They are terrorized, watch him intently, respond instantly to his signal. "I have some delicious salmon for you tonight," he says. He holds the ornate, gilt-embossed menus, does not offer them. They are available if his honored guests choose to examine them, but such perusal, he implies, is unnecessary; *he* will make sure they get the finest of everything. The price, of course, is irrelevant. "Very tender, very young, very fresh," he adds, looking at Lori. "Or perhaps mademoiselle would prefer my roast pork." Not even the chef, it seems, ranks inclusion in his elevated first person; no "we" or "our," these delicacies are his own, he offers them personally. They settle on the salmon. "And would you perhaps like my Grand Marnier *soufflé* for dessert? . . . Excellent! Excellent! And may I suggest my '66 *Le Montrachet* for the salmon?" He's pushing me rather far, Charles thinks. "Bring us the 1970 *Corton Charlemagne*," Charles says. After a slight pause Henri makes the best of it. "A superb

choice, sir. That wine is now at its very peak. Great . . .
style," he adds with a glance at Lori. "Yes, it will com-
plement my salmon very well. Excellent. A superb
choice." This is going to cost an arm and a leg, Charles
thinks. But worth it . . . if it gets her into bed. "To us,"
he says, raising his martini. He drinks, she sips.

Henri snaps his fingers, issues his orders like a symphony conductor with slight hand movements. Throngs
of young black-suited Filipinos swarm around the table,
unfold their napkins, spread them on their laps, pour
water, rearrange the silver, replace the knives for meat
with knives for fish, adjust the flowers.

Lori frowns.

"Are you bothered," Charles asks, "at so much hovering?"

"What?"

"At all this unnecessary attention?"

"Oh . . . no, I don't mind."

Perhaps she has not even noticed. Charles finishes his
martini, hers is hardly touched. Hoping to amuse her,
he talks about the psychology of the maître d'. She seems
distracted, is not really listening. Presently she catches
his eye with a piercing stare, interrupts him in mid-sen-
tence with a solemn announcement: "I think he was talking about me."

"Who?"

"Dr. Melville."

"Oh . . . the lecture. Funny," Charles adds ironi-
cally, "I thought he was talking about me."

"You?"

"Error of narcissism, no doubt. I defer to your claim."

"I'm sure he meant me," Lori says. "He spoke of an analysis that fails because the patient won't talk. You talk, don't you?"

"Pretty much I guess. Too expensive to be silent."

"I'm silent most of the time. He has to fish for everything. If he didn't ask I'd never say a word. Hold everything back. He must get awfully tired of that. Tired of me. And bored. I don't know why he has put up with me so long."

"Maybe he's got a crush on you."

Lori is startled. "You think so?"

"Why not? I do."

"Well, I don't know. Anyway, I'm a terrible patient. Any other analyst would have given up. Long ago. Thrown me out. I can't imagine now why I've been so silent. It seems like stubbornness. When I think of it now it doesn't seem so hard to talk. While I was listening to him this afternoon it suddenly seemed easy. I couldn't believe I had put up such resistance."

Vichysoisse is served. Lori will not stop talking, eats little. At every pause Charles tries to shift her attention from her analyst to him, to the moment, to what he hopes is beginning to happen to them. To no avail. Shrimp salad is served. Henri brings the *Corton Charlemagne*, sniffs the cork; "A masterpiece," he says. When Charles indicates acceptability he pours with a flourish.

"I think everything is going to be different now," Lori says. "From now on I will talk."

"I can believe it," Charles says.

"Wasn't it a magnificent lecture!" Lori exclaims.

As she has already said this several times, Charles merely

nods. Dr. Melville's presence is making him weary. Who invited him? Why is he horning in? Go find your own girl! I'm paying for this dinner. He longs for intimate conversation, romantic ambience, mounting sexual expectation.

At a finger movement from Henri a waiter removes Lori's martini, the glass still full. It's going to be hard to get this girl drunk, Charles thinks. "Lori, do please try the wine. It's quite special." He lifts his glass. "I'm so happy to be alone with you. I love to look at you. To us!"

She takes a sip, begins telling him how Dr. Melville has supported her piano studies, suggested a wonderful teacher. Might as well be jug wine from Safeway, Charles thinks. The salad plates are removed, the fish and vege-tables arrive in covered silver dishes. Three waiters serve them, every movement a flourish. Every few minutes a waiter refills Charles's glass, Lori's glass remains untouched. The salmon is excellent. "Very young, very tender, very juicy," Charles says, hoping to divert Lori's attention with Henri's leer. It doesn't register; she nods and continues with Dr. Melville's empathy, his sensitiv-ity, his understanding, his intelligence. A second bottle of wine is brought, unordered, opened before it arrives at the table: Henri's retaliation for Charles's having declined the Le Montrachet. Charles is irked, realizing that Henri is counting on him not to object because, as Henri knows, Charles is trying to make it with Lori. Trying in vain, Charles thinks morosely. The competition is too stiff. What the hell. He accepts the second bottle, drinks, extends his legs under the table, searches for Lori's legs, finds them. She accepts his touch; does not return the insinuating pressure, but does not withdraw. Charles is encouraged. But not greatly encouraged, because, even as he gently rubs her calf, she still will not shift her attention to him, but explains why analysis would not have worked for her with any other analyst; her resistance, she explains again, is simply too great.

Charles is getting drunk. No, he corrects himself, he is already drunk. The Grand Marnier *soufflé* arrives. One of the young waiters, in his haste to serve it at the perfect moment, burns himself. Badly. Having picked up the oven-hot dish, he had the choice of dropping it on the floor or of holding it in his bare hands until a place was cleared. He held it. A measure of his fear of Henri. Very well. The guests are spared a mess. A glance from Henri informs him, further, that the guests are to be spared, also, his pain. He continues as if nothing has happened.

The *soufflé* is superb. The wine is finished. With Henri's compliments they are served Grand Marnier liqueur. The check arrives. Charles delivers the mortgage to his house, they are free to go.

In the foyer Charles holds Lori's coat as she turns her back to him. Her arms slip into the sleeves. For a moment she is motionless, then leans against him. He closes his arms around her. She turns, still in his arms, smiles happily.

"Thank you for holding my coat. I'll tell you something about that. Oh Charles, I'm happy to be with you tonight. You're the only person I could talk to."

"May I come home with you?"

"Oh yes!"

IN bed she wanted to be close, to snuggle, and to talk. She quickly turned from his kiss on her mouth—it interfered with talking—but seemed happy to be kissed elsewhere, and as he mouthed about her neck and hair and nose and ears she told him about Dr. Melville's helping her with her coat, that it made her strangely, mysteriously, uncomfortable, and that she had lost altogether the memory of his helping her *into* her coat, remembered only his getting her *out* of it, and all that this implied about her unconscious desires.

Meanwhile Charles was stroking the long slender thighs, moving upward, exploring the springy bush, encountering no resistance until he introduced a finger into her cleft, began to follow it between her legs. The thighs clamped shut, "No, not that," she said matter-of-factly, pushing aside his hand.

He retreated, resumed his campaign more cautiously. There was a faint light from the windows, the room was warm; he pushed down the covers, pulled up her gown. Gingerly, but she made no objection. He surveyed the glimmering figure, was suddenly awed by her beauty, was both exhilarated and humble. This great good fortune was undeserved, he was touched by her nakedness and trust. He thought of his wife, her lumpy figure, was then upset at having brought her into such hopeless comparison. There was no place for her here, he tried to put her away in a haven, resumed his stroking of Lori's thighs. To his surprise she lifted her right leg vertically. "Beautiful!" he murmured, tempted to take advantage of the opening, the momentary unwariness, but thought better of it, continued his patient stroking of the now elevated

leg while she told him of that hour when she had been
so paralyzed with resistance the only way Dr. Melville
could get her through it was by having her raise her leg.
Charles moved up on her, massaged her neck, which she
seemed to like, stroked her sides, kissed her breasts and
her belly, played with the short black hair, murmured
about the excellence of each part, but whenever he went
for the center the thighs would clamp shut and she would
push him away. He would then retreat to the periphery
of his target and begin once more his circumspect
approach. She talked while he worked. On and on she
went about their analyst while he plodded away trying to
set fire to this unresponding flesh. To no avail. The friendly
naked body was sibling, not lover. Her immunity to his
desire was causal and absolute.

Suddenly, like a water spigot, her loquacity was turned
off. "That's enough, Charles, I have to sleep. I want to
be fresh for my hour tomorrow." Charles groaned, thinking of how he would feel tomorrow. Lori rolled over on
her side, sighed, began a slow and deep breathing, was
soon asleep.

With the waning of desire Charles felt the impact of
alcohol. He was burning up, his mouth like paper, his
eyes aching and shrunken, a stabbing pain in his head.
He went to the bathroom, drank water; wandered into the
living room, looked down on the late-night lights of North
Beach. Beside him a grand piano gleamed in the reflected
glow. A piece of music stood open on the stand. He could
not read the title.

———————

"MR. MORGAN!" Dr. Melville stood in the open door. "Mr. Morgan!" Waited. No response. Called again, then went down stairs and looked in the waiting room. Mr. Morgan was asleep. "Time for your hour." Still no response. Dr. Melville entered the room, stood before the sleeping man who was sprawled in a chair, one leg straight before him, the other bent back as if broken. One shoe was untied, dragging a long lace. Collar open, shirt and jacket wrinkled. Unshaven, his skin yellowish. His head, over-extended, rested against the wall; he breathed with a rattling snore, Adam's apple bobbing strenuously. His cheeks were sunken, as if without teeth, his eyes slightly open. Dr. Melville touched his shoulder, shook him slightly.

"What! What!" The eyes came blearily open.

"Time for your hour."

"What! . . . Oh, all right." He struggled upright, staggered up the stairs and into the office, fell on the couch. Silence. "I'm going to sleep again," he murmured presently. "Wake me when it's time to go."

"What happened to you?"

Silence. Presently he got up, went to the bathroom. Dr. Melville heard him drink several glasses of water, then wash his face. Returning, he lay down again, sighed. "What happened to me. . . . Good question. What the hell *did* happen to me? I was run over by a truck. Or a train. The 'Twentieth Century Limited.' . . . That's part of the trouble—maybe the whole trouble—that I'm old enough to remember the 'Twentieth Century Limited.' To Chicago. Or the 'Sunshine Special' to St. Louis. Or the 'Sunset Limited' to Los Angeles. Why am I talking about trains? . . . Forgot what I was going to say. Oh, yes. Well . . . anyway, all of them ran over me last night.

"I've been run over by my desire, by my insatiable lust." His speech slowed, slurred, became a rhetorical drawl. "I have the desire of a twenty-year-old, backed up by an imagination, unequalled at any age, with which to envision the most abandoned gratification of that desire. Unfortunately all this superb psychic equipment is housed in the body of an old man. I've been run over by a twenty-five-year old girl. Is that clear? I was run over by *your* patient, Doctor—the beautiful Venetian."

Silence.

"What happened?"

He belched, coughed. "Well . . . what happened? I guess that's easy. Nothing. Nothing happened. Zero. Zilch. Actually, I shouldn't knock the old body. Maybe it would have worked O.K. Who knows? It didn't get a chance. Your lovely Venetian has thighs of steel. Nothing—and I mean nothing—could get between them. Naked, she was in armor. That cunt is all yours, Doc. Whenever you're ready. She's saving it for you. I congratulate you. Though I didn't sample it, I have reason to believe it to be first rate. Congratulations. You're the winner. I take off my codpiece to you!"

He belched again, had a coughing fit. "My body fails me in that I can't handle two lousy bottles of wine. I'm over the hill."

He stood up. "Excuse me."

Dr. Melville heard him, in the bathroom, retch several times then vomit. The flushing toilet. The sound of water in the basin as he rinsed his mouth. His face, when he returned, was ashen; he fell on the couch, groaned.

Silence. Sighs. More groans.

"Now I have to go home. Amelia will be waiting, watching. From a window. I won't see her, but she will see me; the door will open as I lift my hand for the latch. Her face . . . large, pale . . ." he hesitated, his voice lowered, ". . . horsey . . . will be grave, lined with worry. Bad night for her too. She will not have slept. But won't complain, won't scold, will not ask where I have been or what happened. I'm not even sure she would want to know, might not listen were I to tell her. Which I won't.

"Either you express some aggression or you're a martyr. Amelia is a martyr. She doesn't know about anger, doesn't feel it. With an angry woman, some of the time, you could win. With a martyr you always lose. Serves me right for picking such a woman. I grew up in fear of the Commandant, of the pointed finger, the fierce eyes, the denunciation that makes you wither up and die. That's why I searched out Amelia. I was looking for a wife who would never accuse, never complain, never make me feel guilty. Little did I know! There's no safe-conduct through the realm of guilt.

"She will look me over. Survey the damage. She will have chicken soup on the stove, hot and ready. Oh God, chicken soup!" He retched, started to get up, fell back again, continued in a monotone. "She will realize I can't eat. Will take off my shoes, help me undress . . . and into bed. Will bring tea and aspirin. And I will sleep, and when I wake, *then* the soup, and so on and on. Meekly, selflessly, she will nurse me back to guilt-ridden health. . . . Shit!"

Silence. More belching.

"Well . . . I guess that about wraps it up. Nothing more to say. Maybe *you* want to talk today? . . . No? . . . Of course, maybe I'm just resisting. By the way, how come you don't use any of those special techniques of yours on *my* resistance? I pay full fees, don't I? How come I don't get the same treatment? Don't you want me to raise *my* leg?" His right leg shot up in the air, stayed there, the long shoelace dangling wildly. He twisted his head around, grinned balefully. "How about that, Doc, does it give you a thrill? Stir up your unconscious homosexuality? Or is that all analyzed away?" The leg dropped heavily. "Well, I don't blame you for preferring Lori's legs. I do too. I was pawing over them all night, trying to pry them apart." He paused, "Ah!" then an intake of breath, heartfelt appreciation, "They *are* beautiful."

He retched again, his body jerking violently; came upright, sat on the edge of the couch. Groaned. Then, suddenly, "And what about my coat, Doc? It's warm in here. Aren't you going to help me off with it?" He pulled his jacket down off his shoulders, struggled with exaggerated effort to get it lower. "Well! Aren't you going to help me? Can't you see how hard it is, trying to get the coat off? Never mind about getting it on again. I can handle that, but I really need your help in getting if *off*—because of what that symbolizes. . . . To my unconscious, I mean!

"Oh I really got the low-down on you, Doc. Of course you might say I'm just acting out my sibling rivalry, but," he grinned maliciously, "I say I'm not getting a square deal here. Why didn't I go to a pretty woman analyst? Or is that a contradiction of terms?"

He groaned, fell back on the couch. "I'm dizzy when I sit up, dizzy when I lie down." He retched. "This is sour grapes. You don't have to tell me. I'm sore because she prefers you. She's out of her head if you ask me . . . but nobody's asking me."

The buzzer sounded, indicating the arrival of the next patient. "There she is now. All yours. You'll find her in good shape, Doc. Fresh as a daisy. Nothing like me. She didn't drink a thing. I drank *all* the wine. She slept like a kitten. I gotta hand it to you. You have made quite a conquest. This is one helluva racket, this psychoanalysis. Sure beats writing. Wish I could eavesdrop on the next hour, see your tender greeting.

"But are you sure . . . ? Don't misunderstand. I think your technique is terrific. I'm green with envy. Don't misunderstand. But what about your colleagues? Would they really approve of what you've been doing with her? What about the American Psychoanalytic Association? Don't they have an Ethics Committee? Or some sort of Board of Standards? What would they think?"

He sat up, grinned. "Better watch yourself, Doc."

V I ✐ ○.

The Precipice

As Lori entered the office she gave Dr. Melville a strange and, as it were, significant look, looked also about the room, lay on the couch. Silence.

She feels different, she said presently. The room seems different. Everything seems different. She will never be the same again. She was not wearing the usual pants and blouse, but a dark red dress with a small design in black of apples. Was restless, moved about on the couch. It was a magnificent talk. It opened her eyes to many things. Maybe to more than she knows. She has let her freedom slip away. She can see that now. "By not taking responsibility for my actions. For what I fail to do as well as what I do in fact do."

Her voice had changed. She was declaiming.

"You were talking about me. I'm sure. The analysis that fails because the patient won't talk. That must be me." She had told Charles. He was very amusing. She has been thinking about her resistance, how silent she has been. It was only because Dr. Melville had asked questions that she was able to say anything. Held everything back. He must have gotten awfully fed up. Tired of her. And bored. She doesn't know why he has put up with her for so long. "Charles said maybe you . . . have a crush on me. I was shocked. But then, as I thought about it . . . it began to seem possible."

This last was quite unlike her, Dr. Melville thought. Forward, unabashed.

"Anyway," she went on, "you must have been thinking about me. Things are going to be different now. . . . Charles took me to dinner. I suppose he told you. He was making a pass . . . I couldn't stop thinking about you . . . what you had said. That's when it suddenly seemed easy to talk. I couldn't understand why I had been so silent, so difficult, so stubborn. And I couldn't understand, either, why . . . how . . . it had gone away. And so sudden. Something in what you said, but I don't know what. Anyway it's gone. That's why I feel like a different person. I talked all evening to Charles. All night. I talked. He listened. He was very nice."

"How do you feel about Charles?"

"I like him."

"Anything more?"

"No."

"Then why did you spend the night with him?"

Silence. Dr. Melville sensed her becoming defensive. "He *wanted* to."

"I know. But what did *you* want?"

"I was keyed up. I wanted to talk."

"But in bed? Isn't that rather teasing?"

"Well . . . yes . . . I suppose so. I wasn't thinking. You're right. I owe him an apology."

"Maybe, but that's not the point. I'm wanting to know what's happened to you. Why are you behaving this way?"

"I don't know. I feel different. The lecture . . ."

"What about the lecture?"

"I feel free."

"Or perhaps giddy?"

"What do you mean?"

"Intoxicated."

"I drank very little."

"There are other kinds. You are drunk on my lecture." She laughed. "You're right."

"Don't take it lightly. It's not good."

"Why not? I'm sure it is!"

"It's too sudden. Good changes come about slowly, in continuity with the past. They look back at what they are replacing as well as forward at what they are becoming."

"I love the way you talk!"

Dr. Melville found himself clenching his jaw. "You are not yourself today," he said emphatically. "You are a deeply private person, reserved; last night, suddenly, you become a fountain of volubility."

"I wanted to. I'm tired of being reserved. Reserved for what? I want to take more chances."

"You've had a lot of opportunities in the past two years, have turned them all down. Last night you go to bed with a virtual stranger. Why?"

"It wasn't sexual."

"Oh but it was! For him overwhelmingly, infuriatingly sexual. For you, a rehearsal."

"What do you mean?"

"You went to bed with Charles because he is my patient—a stand-in for me."

She fell silent, seemed to turn away from something. "Anyway, I couldn't be alone last night. I was too keyed up. I had to talk."

Dr. Melville had given her pause, but briefly. Now she broke loose, was off again, told him of their dinner, of Charles going home with her, of his efforts in bed. The words spilled out in a rush, full of physical details usually avoided. Dr. Melville was astonished, also uneasy. It seemed unnatural, forced. At the end of the hour he opened the door; she started out, hesitated.

"I've saved the hardest till last," she said. "Is it too late? May I take a minute?"

"Of course." He closed the door.

She glanced down, then lifted her head, looked in his eyes. "I love you." There was a shocked silence. Dr. Melville's ears were ringing. A pistol shot in a quiet room. "No, don't speak!" she added quickly, and for just a moment touched, very lightly, his arm with her hand, and that touch seemed to release, or to convey, her perfume which then enveloped him. "There's not time. Wait." She glanced at the couch, tossed her head as if to get free of something. "It's the closeness of that couch that . . . makes it hard to say. But I'm not . . . afraid any more. That's what I took from your talk. It's *my* feeling, and if it's important I have to stand up for it."

The ring of a prepared speech! She had been rehearsing it last night while Charles—poor Charles!—was pawing away at her. There were minute beads of perspiration under her eyes. The eyes were locked on his, their expression frightened, wild.

"I'm prepared to have you call it . . . transference," she went on jerkily. "That's your trade. But you may as well be prepared for my . . . disagreeing with you." Her breathing was labored, uneven. As if she had to remind herself. She sighed. Her expression became imploring. "That's why I waited: I wanted to tell you like this . . . standing up . . . looking at you. It's too important to throw . . . throw away from the couch."

Dr. Melville started to speak, but was unable, unready. If too important for the couch, it was too important certainly for the doorway. "We'll talk about it tomorrow," he said, rather lamely. She smiled and was gone.

THE next day, as her hour approached, Dr. Melville felt himself in danger. He was relieved, therefore, (also, he noted, a bit disappointed) to find her in a withdrawn mood. She entered the room slowly, glanced about, hesitated, seemed uncertain whether to lie on the couch or sit in the chair. She looked at her analyst enigmatically, then slowly took off her shoes, lay on the couch.

"This is going to be . . . hard. I have a lot . . . of fantasies. I never tell you. They come and go. I don't think about them. Yesterday was . . . different. Right away I knew I would have to tell you. No, not *have* to, want to. I *want* to be free . . . to say anything. Everything. I *want* not to be ashamed.

"So . . ." She paused, took a deep breath. "We go to the opera together. *Der Rosenkavalier*. Perhaps the opening. Very elegant. You are in black. I wear a long dress . . . lavender, flowing. The performance is marvelous. We have a wonderful time. Afterwards a late supper. Then we come to my place. We are very gay. I begin to play the music we have just heard. You sit before me, watching."

Her voice was hoarse, rasping. There was an agitation about her, a recurrent lifting of her head, twisting of pelvis, movement of limbs, trembling of hands. She was as if possessed, or as if reading lines. She sighed, fell silent for a bit.

"I thought of this session, of telling you all this. I went into the bedroom, stood before a mirror. I knew already what I wanted to do. Wasn't sure I would do it. It would be awfully hard to . . . talk about. But then suddenly I knew I *would* tell you. I felt defiant. I mulled it over . . . what I wanted to do. Then went on to do it. Two things: acting out the fantasy . . . as I intended, and at the same time, in imagination . . . telling it to you today . . . as I am now . . . bringing you into it. Watching it together, holding hands."

She had some trouble describing an arrangement of two blouses and a jacket, began to stammer. "Can you picture that? . . . It's complicated." For a moment her natural voice came back, shy, hesitant; but then she went on in her new and driven way. Like a plow, tearing open a virgin turf, cutting roots, turning up slugs. Dr. Melville had the sense that nothing could stop her. Rapidly now, without a pause, she described the imagined seduction, culminating in orgasm as the hand costumed as his touched her vulva.

THAT night Dr. Melville dreams that, having been blocked, he has broken free, has written a paper. He is delighted. It is already in print. There it is before him, in a journal. He looks eagerly to see what he has written, is disappointed that he can't read it, the print is too small. But the title, in gothic letters, is clear:

FOUR UGLY KINGS AND
THREE THEORIES OF NIGHT

Near the title is a small blackish illustration, the head of a crowned and bearded king against a dark background. Perhaps "King Saul" by Rouault. As he looks, baffled, the title becomes sinister. It is urgent that he read the text. He strains his eyes, fumbles for his glasses.

He wakes. Hasn't a clue. His unconscious has thrown up a warning he can't heed.

SOMETIMES it can happen, having foolishly been playing at the edge of a precipice, a mile-high face of merciless granite, at such a place having been playing around, having stumbled and fallen—sometimes it can happen, even so, that for a few crucial moments one will bounce and tumble and scrape against the topmost rocks and projections, one's fall being slowed thereby, just enough to catch a bit of bush growing out of a crack, meager and wobbly, perhaps the last outgrowth before the vertical drop, and it holds—the granite is not completely merciless!— and from that desperate let claw one's way back to safety, quivering, anguished, but alive.

He didn't have to call for her, nor even look in the waiting room; she was standing outside his door, bursting in the moment it was opened, radiantly beautiful, smiling, threw herself on the couch, began a rambling, excited, and euphoric talk; then, suddenly, in the middle of a sentence, fell silent.

"Why am I lying on this couch?" She sat up abruptly. "I don't want to be on this couch. Not for a very long time have I wanted to be on this couch. Didn't have the . . . the nerve to say so. I don't want to be your patient. In fact, I am *not* your patient. I'm stopping. Right now. I *have* stopped." She got up, took two or three strides in the room, turned, came back, stood before his chair, loomed over him. "Our professional relationship is over. I feel wonderful. I feel free." She raised her arms over her head, body arched like a bow, as if offering her breasts. "I should have done this a long time ago. For weeks this hasn't really been analysis. For months . . ."

"Stop! You are . . ."

"Don't you know what this has been? Our relationship? A stifled love affair."

She sat before him on the ottoman, coming down so suddenly he barely got his feet out of the way. He was alarmed to find her face so close. The eyes were enormous, her mouth larger than he had thought. She wore dark eye shadow; and the analyst in him, detached even under siege, came up with a surprising thought: that bluish purple is meant, unconsciously, to suggest the pigmented labia. It's a promise! The eyes you can see now, the rest later. She wore a tight silk dress, jungle print, large design, green and black and scarlet. Passion flowers. As she sat, the dress came above her knees which were but a hair's breadth from his own. Stockings, high heels, fragile filmy shoes. She leaned toward him; the long curved lashes seemed to sweep his face, her breath was on his cheek. She smiled. The red lips parted. He shrank back. What large teeth you have, Grandmother! Now there's an association! What should he do? His thoughts were scampering about wildly, like mice in a cage. She was diving into his eyes, deeply, had taken them over as her private pools. She was so close! Her gaze was like glue, was sucking out his essence. Is this what it feels like, to be a sexual object? He squirmed about, trying to extricate himself, to stand up. She was leaning toward him, her knees pressing his, he couldn't move. He must break free! He closed his eyes, put up his hands, surged forward, bumping against her. She almost fell off the ottoman, caught his arms.

Somehow he struggled to his feet carrying her with him, raised his hand in a gesture of warding her off. "Wait a minute!" he pleaded, but she was not to be put off. She stood facing him, beaming on him the burning radiance of her new-found happiness, fierce in her determination to protect it. She smiled, threw back her head, raised her arms, and slowly, ecstatically, combed long fingers through the glistening hair. He found himself enveloped in her perfume. Chlöe. His favorite. And now—dizzy, breathless, hanging still on the sheer face of that cliff—came another crazy association: Perfume is meant to be perceived—since only women wear it—as emanating from that part of a woman's body which differs from man's. The odor is about the neck and ears but is meant to be sensed as drifting up from below. "This is the smell of my cunt." That's the message. "Do you like it? Go ahead. Sniff me!" The male dog sniffs the rear end of the bitch. Women arrange that we get the same information, more delicately, though less reliably, by sniffing their necks.

He doesn't know how it happened. Perhaps a moment's lapse. Her arms were around him, he felt her breasts against his chest, his hands rested on her waist. Her soft and slightly open lips were moving slowly on his own, back and forth, round and round, pressure gradually increasing, her tongue making itself known, tenderly, teasingly, promisingly, advancing slightly, flying away again. He was spinning, slipping, it was now or never. The valley floor glimmered far below, the bush was giving way. Another moment and they would be in free fall.

He pushed her violently away.

She staggered back, just avoiding a table, regained her balance. He yelled at her: "Stop!" He scowled, wiped his face. "I have some things to say to you." He maintained the heaviest, most authoritarian, tone he could muster. "You have got to listen. And think. Think hard. Because this isn't going to be easy." Her face softened, a covert smile twitched at her lips, coyness came to her eyes. She lowered her gaze, the long lashes sweeping downward, folded her hands. Oh God, he thought, she thinks this is part of the game. "Sit down," he said, a little softer.

"There." He pointed to a chair some distance away. She sat, docile, waiting. "You cannot . . ." he sought a commanding phrase, "terminate analysis this way. You are still my patient."

"I have stopped," she said blithely. "I am *not* your patient."

"This is crazy, what you're doing. I can't permit it."

"I do it on my own. You can't force me to be your patient."

"No, I can't. And wouldn't want to. But you know . . . and I know . . . that stopping analysis is not the issue. You want to start something else."

"Yes!"

"It's not possible."

Her face clouded. "Why not?"

"It's unethical. It's not fair to you. It would destroy me."

"But if I stop being your patient. . . ? Why is it unethical. . . ?"

"These things take time. You are acting out in the transference. Just saying you're stopping treatment doesn't change that. And does not remove my responsibility not to take advantage of it."

"Take advantage? . . . I don't understand."

Before he could reply she stopped him with an impatient gesture. "Do you love me?"

"I'm not permitted to love you."

"We can *break* the rules. Don't you know that!" Her voice was rising. "Let's *permit ourselves*. Let's *permit each other*. What do we care about the rest?"

He stared at her. In distress she was overwhelmingly

desirable. He was looking at the impossible, but looking from very close. Her skin, her perfume, the touch of her lips, filled his mind, made him dizzy. He tried to speak, felt his mouth take on a silent grimace, shook his head. In his confusion she regained composure, regarded him thoughtfully.

"You're right," she said presently. "This is an . . . an impossible . . ." A wave of her arm took in the office. "This place requires us to be at cross purposes. We want to be somewhere together . . . somewhere . . . but can't get there from here. We have to get somewhere else first. I will get us to that somewhere else."

He shook his head again, and found his voice. "The cross purposes . . . or, anyway, *my* purpose, has to be *meant*. I can't mean it and at the same time accept your help in making sure it fails."

She considered this for a moment, then shrugged. "Let's wait and see." She put out her hand, smiled. A tender look came to her eyes; they were telling him something: This is our last appointment, but life goes on. Something will happen. We will meet again. Trust me.

"No, Lori. What you want is not possible. And I can't let you leave believing I will . . . somehow . . . allow it to happen."

Suddenly she was on the floor, arms around his knees. "I'm offering myself to you. Don't you want me?"

He pulled her up. Her face was desperate. Now *she* was on the edge, a bottomless humiliation beneath her. How could he lend a hand without their falling together?

"Lori . . . I beg you. You're not yourself. Since that lecture you have been possessed . . . a different person.

You talk differently, you walk differently, you dress . . ."
He gestured uncertainly. "Something alien has come over
you. You see it as freedom, and you're happy about it.
Only you're not really happy. It's a false happiness . . .
hectic, hysterical. It's my fault. It's as though I have hypnotized you, and while you were in a deep trance pro-
grammed you to think and feel and say all these things
that you now do think and feel and say. It's not you. It
only *seems* to be you. I see how real it is to you, how
much you feel it . . . and how hard it is for you to believe
me. But it's not real, it won't last, it couldn't last. You've
trusted me in the past, maybe more than you should, but
now, it's terribly important. Trust me now. You must. A
little longer. You have to be patient, to hold still. Nothing can be decided now. You must not stop treatment."

She was staring at him, moving her head slowly from
side to side. "Don't you want me?" she said again.

"You are a . . . a beautiful and . . . desirable woman.
Under other circumstances I . . . think you know how I
would answer. I . . . would say yes. In these circumstances I can't. I simply cannot."

She searched his face wildly. "Don't you love me?"

"I'm not free."

"Don't you want me?"

"Lori! Try to get hold of yourself."

She stared at him with unbelieving horror. Mouth open,
backing away, crouching slightly. A grimace appeared
around her mouth, deepened, her features twisted, the
face crumpled. He saw her fall away down the precipice,
a rising wail as she disappeared from view.

VII ⟋⟋⟋◦

The Prize

THE caller was leaning on the button. Dr. Melville stared down miserably at his drink. No escape. Home is no sanctuary. He stood up uncertainly, looked about the room, now somehow unfamiliar. Cora, fortunately, was out.

Don't let her in . . . not in here, he counseled himself. And don't discuss it at the door. Tell her you will see her tomorrow. He started out of the room. Wait! She is probably in a state. Let me think. If she's frantic . . . if she insists, I'd better see her. But not here, and not right this minute. Tell her to come to the office . . . at eight. Tonight.

He opened the door, faced his angry and distraught patient. There was no doubt about the emergency, Lori was quite hysterical. After a few exchanges he closed the door, poured himself another drink.

LORI'S BMW was parked in front of his office, but she was not there. He waited, became alarmed. At ten o'clock he telephoned her house, no answer. He went outside, found her car to be unlocked, looked through it. No clue. He returned to his office, telephoned Mount Zion Hospital, San Francisco General Hospital, and the police. No record. In his own car he began to cruise the neighborhood. Geary to Fillmore to Bush to Scott. On Sutter near the Psychoanalytic Institute two young men were standing in the street facing the sidewalk, looking down. One of them was laughing. As Dr. Melville came alongside, passing a parked car, he saw a figure on the ground. He circled through the Institute parking lot, came back, brought the two men into his headlights. Lori was sitting on the curb before them, knees up, still in that short wild dress, those filmy shoes, head tilted up, drinking. Leaving the headlights on and the motor running, Dr. Melville got out and went to her. The two men dropped back; then, realizing he was not a cop, moved closer. "For God's sake, Lori! Get up!" He took from her hand a pint bottle of rum.

"Say, man, whatcha doin'?"

They were in their twenties, black. One of them was pudgy, wore an orange t-shirt, had a ragged fringe of wispy beard, a round empty face that glistened in the headlights; the other, the one who spoke, was of lighter color, had thick Afro hair, wore a dangling scarf and a leather jacket.

"She's my daughter," Dr. Melville said firmly, "and she's sick. I'm taking her home. . . . Here, take this." He thrust the bottle at the chubby one who, automatically, took it. "Get up, Lori! Get up!" He put his arm around her, pulled her up.

"Hey, man. Maybe the lady don wanna go."

They were moving in, crowding him. He felt body contact. "Tell them!" he hissed in her ear.

"It's all right," Lori said to them. "I know him." She waved her arm vaguely. ". . . Was nice talking to you."

He got her into the car, slammed the door. The man in the leather jacket raised an arm, they were going to jump him. At that moment a car rounded the corner catching them in the headlights. They hesitated, Dr. Melville jumped in his car, locked the door. There was a thunderous kick on the rear fender as he pulled away, followed a moment later by an explosion of glass as the bottle of rum smashed on the rear window.

He drove to Scott Street, pulled up behind her car in front of his office. "Let's get inside before something else happens." He got out, opened the door for her; she didn't move. "Come on, Lori!" She shook her head. "What's the matter?" She was huddled up, bent over, looking at the floor. He closed the door, got back in the car behind the wheel. Waited. She didn't move. "Are you drunk?"

"I guess so." Her voice was dull and empty.

"We have to talk, Lori. Let's go inside."

She shook her head. "I won't go in there again."

"Why not?"

"I'm crazy. I have to be locked up."

Dr. Melville heard footsteps, in the mirror saw the two men approaching from Sutter Street, about thirty feet away. He started the car, they broke into a run, he pulled away. Again there was a crash of something thrown at the car. He drove Scott to Pacific to Broderick, parked where Broderick dead-ends on Broadway. Lori had taken no heed of this second encounter, still sat motionless looking at her hands. The dim light glinted on a falling tear.

He turned her toward him, held her shoulders. "You're not crazy. You don't have to go to a hospital. You were right. Everything you said. A stifled love affair. You're right. I have fallen in love with you."

She looked up with wide eyes, dusty cheeks ribboned with glistening tracks. He turned away. A chasm opened. No taking it back. The steep hillside, alive with lights, fell away before him. He saw his own house.

Lori touched his arm. "Then we *can* . . ."

"No. That's not possible." Goaded, tormented by powerless desire for something freely offered. He shook his head, became impatient. "I told you . . . this afternoon. I meant it . . . everything."

"But if you . . ."

"No, Lori. No. It's settled. I can't. You can't. We can't."

"But couldn't we . . ."

"No. No."

She became frantic, grabbed his hands. "But you can't just . . . say you love me and then act as if you hadn't said it. You can't *do* that!"

"It was my failure, Lori . . . I . . ."

"Why can't you trust us?"

"*You* have to trust *me*. We must not go further." He felt the doubt beneath his firmness. He was beating her down, was going to prevail . . . then would have to live with his victory. No second chance.

"I won't give up!"

"I want what you want. But wanting is not everything. There are things we can't have."

She stared at him bitterly. "Coward!"

He winced. "I'll take you home. You can pick up your car tomorrow."

"There won't be any tomorrow. I'll get myself home."

She got out, started toward Divisadero Street. He caught her, turned her around. She squared off, knocked his hand from her shoulder.

He became angry. "I take back what I said, Lori: you *are* crazy. You're out of your mind."

"Leave me alone!"

"You can't walk about like this! What are you trying to do? You're asking to be raped or murdered . . . or both."

"It's no longer your concern."

She strode off. He went back to his car, drove after her, slowly, staying about forty feet behind. She glanced back angrily, gesturing for him to go away. In an effort to lose him, she darted into the dark yard of a house, behind a hedge, was met instantly with the furious deep barking of a dog. She emerged on the run, continued on the sidewalk. Down the steep Divisadero hill to Jackson, to Washington, to Clay. Approaching Sacramento Street, a group of three or four men in the intersection, talking, laughing. As she came closer they fell silent, her steps slowed, stopped. Dr. Melville drew alongside, she opened the door and got in. He took her to her car, watched as she drove away.

———

He could not go home. He drove to Lombard Street, took a room in a motel, lay on the bed in the dark, listened to the sounds of traffic, watched the flickering luminescence on the closed curtain of the changing neon street signs.

The mattress was hard, he lay on his back, hands clasped under his head, the ceiling turning rose, then yellow, then violet, violet like her eyes, over and over, rose-yellow-violet, the fog drifting in, and gradually the roar of traffic grew distant, muted, like surf on a receding tide, the luminescence changing, other colors making an appearance, pink and blue, once and then gone, the surf changing in tone, the sound of bells, and far away but coming closer the deep falling note of a foghorn. The room was detached, was floating down Lombard Street, drifting—Gough Street, Octavia, Laguna, Buchanan, Webster, Fillmore—westward to the sea, and again the violet of her eyes, eyes that now, somewhere—where was she? would he ever see her again?—were angry, distraught, weeping. Lombard Street had become a river, he was on a raft, on his back, glazed eyes staring upward, too spent, exhausted, to look ahead to what was coming or to the side to what was passing. It had all begun so harmlessly, he could see her still as on that first time, standing in his doorway, two years ago, awkward, tense, needful, with those big frightened eyes, nothing to him, just another patient, albeit unusually pretty, her entrance into his life making no noise, unremarked in his journal, appearing only in his appointment book, Savella, underlined in red indicating a first visit. No disturbance, no splash, but suddenly there she was beside him in still, deep water, and so they began their drift together, not a controlled trip with an expert guide as she had a right to expect and as he would have liked to think, but for a while a regular dependable drift side by side for an hour a day four days a week, the river bearing them forward, the changing panorama of bank more and more unnoticed so increasingly intent were they on each other— Steiner Street, Pierce, Scott, Divisadero—still water at the start but gradually they began to circle, to move around each other, to spin, were sucked under, and he now thrown up alone in a strange eddy, perhaps never to see her again, the river breaking up in white water over rocks—Broderick, Baker, Lyon—and now faintly the roar of a cataract ahead.

At home Lori swallowed a bottle of pills—all that was left of the Valium—took paper and pen, sat down to write. A stinging indictment. "To Dr. Melville." Suddenly veered. What had she done? She must not give him such satisfaction. No doubt it would suit him just fine that she die. In the bathroom she pushed fingers down her throat, gagged, retched. She telephoned Charles. "I'm in terrible trouble." When she heard his voice she began to cry. "Can you come over?" "Of course." "But you have to promise . . . you won't take me to a hospital?" "Why would I do that?" "Well . . . I'm pretty crazy." But she might lose consciousness before he got there. Better open the door now. When he arrived he found her on the carpeted stair, doubled up in pain.

She was dazed and faint but could stand. He supported

her up the stairs and into the bathroom, held the con-
vulsed body as she vomited, bathed her face and hands,
put her to bed. She was deathly pale, sweat stood out on
her forehead. After a while she slept but moved about,
moaned, talked loudly, unintelligibly, held his hand
tightly. He sat beside her for hours. Her sleep deepened.
He stretched out alongside her, held her hand, listened
to the now regular breathing. He waked to find himself
alone. A gray day, raining. He searched through the flat,
then drove through the maze of North Beach and Telegraph Hill, found her walking on Columbus Avenue at
Bay Street, wearing a raincoat, nothing underneath, san-
dals on her feet, rain running on her face, hair dripping.
"Lori! Get in the car! You're out of your mind!" At home
she had a shaking chill. He dried her hair, rubbed her
body, found a flannel nightgown, gave her hot tea. Again
she slept. When next she waked it was nighttime.

SHE paced the flat and raged. Her father would send
someone to kill him. Charles patted her shoulder, murmured in her ear. She would sue him, spread his name
across the tabloids, seducer of patients. She would destroy
him. No one would ever come to him again. Charles
kissed her wrists, brushed the long fingers with his parted
lips, turned her hands up, kissed the palms. She would
not let him get away with it. Nobody could treat her like
that! Nobody! Charles massaged the small of her back,
caressed her breasts, buried his face in her hair, breathed
her exotic odors. It was so terribly, terribly humiliating.
How could he do such a thing! How could she ever again

hold up her head? She was a princess, Charles told her, carrier of divine fire, and nobody, nothing, could diminish her. But she had made such a fool of herself, she cried, throwing herself at him that way. Unwanted. Rejected. Charles took her on his lap, stroked the long thighs, kissed away the tears.

So the prize that fell from the hands of Dr. Melville landed snugly in the waiting and now strangely tender hands of Charles Morgan, and Lori waked one morning to the realization that what she had sought in vain from her analyst was hers in abundance from the man in her arms.

VIII 〰

Midnight

LORI was in love, was happy, but would not forgive
her analyst. She would never go back to that terrible man.
But she *should* go back, Charles told her. Dr. Melville
was no monster, had meant no harm, was not playing
with her. The humiliation was unintended. He had lost
his heart to her. For an analyst a mistake, to be sure, but
one for which, in view of the overwhelming appeal of
her physical self, to which he had been daily subjected,
she should have forebearance. Indeed, she may have
contributed to the infatuation. No matter that she was
inhibited, blocked; the provocativeness of the shy can be
enormous: that strangled silence, that helplessness, that
faltering glance, the downward sweeping lashes, that
remote and locked-away fire—though not quite so remote
nor so safely locked away as Dr. Melville had thought.
Dr. Melville's lapse need not further concern her; it would
not happen again. He had been scorched by desire,

henceforth would be scrupulously correct. But she ought to be concerned with how *she* had so misjudged the situation. *That* ought to be worked out.

So she came back, and Dr. Melville began to gather up the fragments of her shattered analysis.

"But I *love* him!" Lori protested.

"It feels like love," Dr. Melville said, "but it is not love. It is a compulsion to master the feared and adored father. To subdue him, to possess him, to take him away from your mother. And the object of this drive is not Charles. Charles is a stand-in for me, as I was a stand-in for your father."

"I will not have you telling me what I feel. Or for whom. I know what I feel, and I love him."

"What you feel, like a fire in its urgency, is like an iceberg in its form. What you *see* looks like love. I'm telling you about the larger, the submerged, part, a drama peopled with figures from your past. The puppet show, now so enthralling, will become tedious. You will tire of him."

"Never!"

"We'll see. Wait. Give yourself time."

"Wait for what? I don't want to wait."

"You're acting out."

"Are you quite the right person to teach me about that?"

The shy Venetian had become savage. "My own acting out," Dr. Melville said icily, "has been admitted, is not in question here. The issue is *your* acting out and whether you can control it. . . . But if you mean to imply that I am not qualified to treat you, I will send you to someone who is."

"I won't go to anyone else."

"Then you must deal with what I tell you. You have fabricated an instant and illusory attachment because you could not tolerate the rejection by me. Like a splint for a broken leg. It's a hard time for you, you need all the support you can get. But you're mistaking the splint for a healed and solid bone. It's not healed. It takes time."

"What do you want me to do?"

"Hold still. Don't act on what you feel; examine it."

"Am I not supposed to see him?"

"See him if you like, but don't make too much of it."

"What does that mean?"

"Don't move in with him. Don't start out right away building a foundation under this relationship. Don't begin planning a life together. Not yet."

"It's too late. We're already living together."

"I HAD thought to make a conquest," Charles said to Dr. Melville, "but have fallen in love. The conquest, if there is one, is hers. How strange! A few months ago I was complaining about the degradation of the sexual impulse, love becoming something ugly, predatory, becoming finally just an itch to fuck. That's all gone. I adore her. What we do together, the intimate things, the minglings . . . they take place in mystery, are not carnal but spiritual, even holy. I have become a different man. Younger, idealistic."

"She's young," Dr. Melville said, "so of course *you*

feel young. And beautiful, so you feel also like a con-
queror. And therefore grateful. And this gratitude is perceived as love. And that mystery, that something spiritual
and holy—that's the awe you feel at the miraculous res-
toration of your youth. But she can't really give you youth.
The gift is an illusion."

Long silence.

"While you, Dr. Melville, having escaped but nar-
rowly the dangerous surface of things, are back safely in
the still depths where the storms that would blow us away
may be trivialized as infantile fantasy." He paused, then
added in a lowered voice, "Like an air-traffic controller
in the tower, watching planes take off in a storm, warning
of crashes."

He's right, Dr. Melville thought. Safe in my tower
again, I am being wise about those who act. He felt distaste. There's something shameful about wisdom which
issues from a sanctuary. A gloomy silence filled the room.
Nevertheless, he could see certain things from this tower
which Charles could not, or would not, and, though
remorseful and angry at being there, he felt bound to
report what he saw.

"I do warn of crashes," he said presently. "Particularly
foolish, unnecessary crashes. I'm not challenging your
right to leave your wife . . . if you're unhappy with her.
Maybe you should. It's a difficult decision. It may destroy
her—as it might destroy you to stay with her. Either way
you may be wrong, either way you may come to regret
it. It's your decision. I wouldn't make it for you even
if I could. What I'm telling you now is something
more limited: you should not leave your wife in this

impulsive way or for this particular woman."

"That could be, Doc. But I would think, in view of your own involvement with 'this particular woman'—in view of your being in fact my rival—you might disqualify yourself from offering such advice."

Dr. Melville was stung. "That's awfully sharp . . . but perhaps just. Why don't you . . . go to someone else to talk this through?"

Long silence. "No." Another silence. "I don't trust anybody in this business . . . but maybe I distrust you less than the others."

"Then I must tell you that this is an as-if relationship. She loves you *as if* you were her father. She doesn't know that, she can't tell you, can only deny it, but I know it. She has draped images over you; what you experience as love of you is her response to those images."

The lace curtains stirred gently, the fog drifted in, the gray light rose, filled the room. Dr. Melville spoke from still depths at the bottom of the pool.

"You are, I might add, three years older than her father."

Lori's father and older brother were coming to San Francisco for a visit. Would stay four days. "Will you introduce Charles to them?" Dr. Melville asked.

"Yes, of course."

"As your lover?"

"Well . . . that will be pretty obvious."

"As someone you live with?"

"I suppose so. Would you expect me to hide it?"

"As the man you want to marry? . . . If he gets a divorce?"

"It's too early to talk about that." She was irritated. "Why all these questions?"

"I want to know what you anticipate, how your father will take it. . . . What does Charles think about it?"

"He's nervous . . . but pleased. Wants to meet them."

"Does your father know anything about Charles?"

"No."

"Your mother?"

"No . . . nothing."

"Nothing? Well, isn't this going to be rather an unpleasant shock?"

She became uncomfortable, twisted on the couch. Presently she turned on her side facing the wall, drew up her knees, put her head down, sighed. Then, in a voice that had become very small: "They will just have to accept it."

As the time approached she began to cough, developed a sore throat, could hardly talk. "I can't face it," she said finally to Dr. Melville. "My father will blow up. I know it." She sighed. "What shall I do?"

"Tell Charles it's too early, that you have to wait."

LORI was practicing scales and was bored. Scales bred daydreams, and she would lose her place. It was so tedious! She would shake her head vigorously, back and forth, to fling away the intruding images, would clench her teeth, eyes narrowed in resolve, and for a few minutes all would be well. Then she would lose it. Her mind was at the disposal, not of her intention, but of drifting desires—for fame, love, recognition, acclaim. Something inside, turbulent, clamoring, pressed for utterance. She wanted to compose, then to perform what she had written. Like Chopin or Liszt. She left the piano, stared out the window, thinking, trying to sense the code for translating yearning into music. She couldn't think, felt empty. As in analysis, nothing comes to mind. Maybe reason does not apply. She longed for revelation, a movement directly from feelings to fingers. She went back to the piano, closed her eyes, began to improvise. The sound was mellifluous, gentle. She didn't like it, began a pattern of staccato discords. Like Bartok. No, not exactly. What was it? In itself? Banal. Trivial.

It occurred to her to play an indisputably great work. She opened the volume of Beethoven sonatas, chose the "Hammerklavier," the slow movement, read through it lightly, played transitional passages, then sat up straight, her expression determined and serious, and began to play. She struck deep into the solemn chords, listened intently. What did she hear? Not much. It was disappointing. This music had a complaining tone. Must be the way she was playing it. She put Serkin's recording on the phonograph. He did it better, but the music itself was still self-pitying, was still a bore. She listened then to Brendel's version. No better. This sonata was dead. She went back to the piano, played a Chopin waltz. This sounded silly, giggly. A virus was spreading through the realm of music.

Charles came out of the bedroom where he had been working, smiled at her. "Sounds wonderful!" His eyes were watery, his glasses pushed up on his forehead. His forehead seemed longer, more sloping, as if his hair had retreated overnight. He had that relaxed, expended air which meant his work had been going well, that he was "written out," was tired, content, hungry. He would want to talk now, to have a drink, to eat. He came up behind her at the piano, put his arms around her. "And how is my muse? My beautiful—nay, more than beautiful—my ravishing muse?" She didn't want to be his muse. She envied his spent state, his relaxed emptiness, his languor; he had given birth, she was blocked. "Why can't you be *my* muse?" she said. He laughed genially, which further irritated her. "I would if I could, but hardly have the figure for it! While you—" he slipped his hands inside her blouse, found her braless, "Ah, wonderful!—are marvelously equipped.

"A full handful," he went on, whispering in her ear, "one for each hand, silky smooth, warm, soft, each with a special crown or summit from which"—he caressed her nipples—"on occasion, upon proper approach and invitation, will emerge promontories of bliss." The nipples came erect but she felt nothing. His right hand slipped down to her belly, his teeth were nibbling at her ear. But he's nice, she thought, and it's good to be wanted. She turned around in his arms, kissed him on the mouth, his hand moved to her thigh.

The virus was spreading. His hands on her body, what he was doing, what would come—all that was known, familiar, might even be pleasant, yet would also, she knew in advance, be empty. Background music, but nothing in the foreground. Where was the main theme, where was life itself?

Suddenly her skin recoiled at his touch. A shudder of revulsion swept through her. She restrained an impulse to push him away.

ONE evening Cora appeared at dinner with a regular grid of punctate lacerations on her left cheek. The explanation she offered, whatever it was, passed muster with Dr. Melville. But not, as it happened, for long. Psychoanalysts enter upon triply guarded secrets. In this instance it proved to be Cora's great discretion that led to her precise identification: she would not permit her lover to call her at home, the ensuing argument led to a fight, he followed her into the kitchen and hit her finally with the first thing at hand, which happened to be a grater. Whereupon he felt so guilty and upset that he went to talk to Dr. Azulman, a clinical psychologist recommended to him by a driver for United Parcel. Dr. Azulman, still in training, was having his work supervised by Dr. Angus Fortman, a third-year candidate at the Psychoanalytic Institute, who, in turn, happened to be in training analysis with Dr. Henry Melville. Dr. Fortman, caught up just now in negative transference which he could not bring himself to express, and, in this state of resistance, casting about for something to say, that is for something without any emotional significance, simply reported the case that Dr. Azulman had just reported to him. Thus Dr. Melville heard about a woman named Cora whose lover had hit her in the face with a grater last Thursday afternoon on Potrero Hill.

After thinking it over, Dr. Melville decided he didn't

care. Indeed, that evening, sitting side by side with Cora watching television—the greater wounds, he observed, were healing nicely—he felt it might be better this way. His conflicts were characteristically resolved in favor of fear rather than of impulse, with the result that his was a life of duties rather than of gratifications, and this new development somehow left him lighter, less obligated. But also strangely sad, restless, full of longing.

A storm was underway. Rain was drumming against the house, streaming down the dark panes. Trees were whipping about in the high wind. He drove to the foot of Telegraph Hill, walked up the curving road through driving rain. Gusts would surge and push him back, threaten to blow him down, followed by lulls in which he could hear the dripping from trees and houses, the rush of runnels in gutters.

He found her house near the top, an old Victorian that had been rebuilt. Narrow and deep, two flats, hers the upper. Lighted entrance. Through the glass door, thickly carpeted stairs leading up. Brass numbers. Lighted bell. Polished brass hardware. He stood there, dripping, thinking. So this is the door through which she comes and goes. To grocer, to baker, to music teacher. Here she leaves at one-forty in the afternoon to come to me. And here she returns at three-fifteen. Up and down those stairs her ankles cross each other, scissoring back and forth. Home. This is where she plays the piano, where she sleeps, where she eats. Home, also, these last months, to Charles Morgan. The door through which he, too, comes and goes. From which he, too, leaves to come to me . . . and returns to her. Here they sit down together, here they

make love, here sleep in each other's arms. On that fate-
ful day, if I had chosen differently—and I was within a
hair's breadth!—this would now be home to me, and not
to him. Charles, not I, would be out in the rain. In my
pocket would be the key to this lock. I would know it by
touch, would open and close this door with the easy
unthinking motions of one who lives here, would enter
and leave as a familiar, would climb those stairs, would
bound up those stairs to her who waits. Would clasp her
to me . . .

It's all an illusion. It couldn't be. It wouldn't last. It
won't last for Charles Morgan. Would no more for me.
. . . But for a while! Yes! For a while it would. A few
weeks. Months. Maybe that ought to be enough. Why
must I always go for permanence? What in life is per-
manent? That's the illusion. Maybe the best things are
brief, all missed by me, lost, lost, all of them, because of
opting always for the long run. Long run to what? To
death. Why not see Naples and die? Who's to say that
that's the wrong way?

He was startled by a sound, turned to see an old woman,
arm outstretched, moaning, lurching toward him. She
wore a black knitted cap from which white hair, stringy,
dripping water, fell down to her shoulders. Her features
were large. The street light overhead cast stark and tragic
shadows on her contorted face. Perhaps she had slipped,
was averting a fall. She recovered, passed on without a
word, disappeared up the hill.

I shouldn't be standing here, he thought. Lori might
come down those stairs. Any moment. Or he. Or both
of them. Or maybe they're not home. But may arrive any

minute. Car stopping. Right here. Beside me. Doors opening. Both of them getting out. Astonished. Their analyst, forlorn at their door in the storm. And what would I say?

I am for them the guardian of standards, of norms. A living symbol of the belief that there is a sensible way to live and a sick way to live, and that the two can be reliably distinguished one from the other. So what then am I doing at their door at midnight? . . . Thinking sick is better, that's what. And would I tell them that?

The lull had passed. The wind again was whipping his coat tails, lashing the trees back and forth. Rain drove in at his collar, trickled down his back. His coat was drenched, he felt his shirt getting wet. Holding his hat, he started back down the hill. The road curved around, and presently he could look back and up to the windows of their flat. Glass walls floor to ceiling, lights on. A form appears. Is it she? Another. The two forms stand close together, perhaps looking out at the storm. Do they embrace? The driving wind bends a tree, holds it down, blocks his view. When it is released the light is out. He stares at the black windows. Rain runs down his arms and legs. They will be going to bed now. . .

So there they are, he thinks, together, warm in each other's arms, in their neuroses, in their acting out; and here am I, desolate, storm-swept, alone, in my mental health, my splendid adjustment.

LORI was bored, intensely restless, would flounce into Dr. Melville's office, seductive, flamboyant, hysterical.

She had stopped practicing, spent much time with Jerry, an agent who wanted to get her into acting. From Charles, Dr. Melville heard that she was falling in love with Jerry, was probably already having an affair.

"She's with him all the time," Charles said. "He wants to take her to New York. And I think she wants to go. But won't say. Because of me, I suppose. But more and more it seems like obligation rather than love. If I could afford to be honest, and I'm not sure I can, I'd say I'm holding her back."

From Lori, however, Dr. Melville got a different impression. She spoke lightly of Jerry, often with contempt, treated the matter of becoming an actress as a lark. She was simply playing around, she said. It was something to do. She couldn't be serious all the time. He was of course trying to get her in bed, but she did not respond, he wasn't her type. Charles was making her uncomfortable with his mute reproaches. She became defiant, began to read feminist tracts, became argumentative, they began to have fights. She joined a women's group in Berkeley, went to meetings twice weekly. Sometimes the group would meet at her flat on Telegraph Hill. Eight or ten women, mostly older than she, in their thirties, pants, short hair, intense, awkward. Their voices would reach Charles in the bedroom, would make him uncomfortable. On the occasion of a routine check-up Lori switched to a woman gynecologist recommended by her group. They recommended, also, a female psychotherapist, but she demurred.

There was something brittle and provocative in her manner. Her gait had changed; in the past meditative, now it was brisk. It brooked no nonsense, particularly no male nonsense. She was altogether turned off sexually. Sex was a bore, was vastly overrated, it made her sick. She spoke in a scornful, impatient manner, was full of complaints about Charles.

"Aren't you," Dr. Melville said, "ignoring your own part in this? Your coldness toward him?"

She fell silent, her body tensed, the air suddenly thick with defensiveness. Dr. Melville, considering the consequences, did not insist. She was acting out with Jerry an ulterior purpose, was provoking Charles to leave her. She could not herself leave him, but neither could she stay, her body revolted, she could hardly bear for Charles to touch her.

HE needed to be alone, Charles told her. For a while. He had to go home. Unfinished business. No, he couldn't do it with her. Some things, to be done at all, must be done alone. Ghosts will not appear for a committee.

She didn't believe him, but, he observed, did not look straight in his eyes as when seeking the truth. Her gaze was restless, averted. He was holding her in his arms; her eyes, close to his own, were large, glistening, violet. They snatched up a pain in his heart. One can't possess something like that, he thought, so beautiful, so wild. Possession is illusion. One must let go. In those eyes he now saw a furtive hope, warded off, but not altogether. She wanted to be convinced.

He was beginning a new work, he told her. A long work. But it was not secure. The vision was elusive, was hiding, teasing him, permitting of itself but occasional glimpses. Might drift away, vanish altogether. He had to be patient, coax it close in clear light. A waiting game, a hide-and-seek. The hunter in the blind must wait alone.

She wants to believe. She sighs, she presses his hand. She believes.

I X

The Corner

AFTER Charles left, Lori stopped seeing Jerry, resumed piano lessons, began practicing long hours. Though never again so inhibited as at the beginning of her analysis, the old shyness came back. And that aura of mystery as she entered and as she left the office, that mingling of gaze which was like a fusion of souls, a silent contract whereby they agreed that, while many important things may be said, the deepest things are to be but evinced and inferred. Dr. Melville felt in her slight smile, in the startled and furtive yearning of those violet eyes, something that clutched up his heart.

One day, at that moment of most intimate contact, just as he opened the door for her, they ran into his next patient, waiting, blocking the door, beginning to talk. The encounter was awkward, Lori fled down the stairs. The next day she was silent, could think of nothing.

"I know why you are sad," Dr. Melville said.

He observed her breathing, which had been jerky and shallow, become deep and regular: she knew he was going to talk to her, she began to relax.

"After we say good-by at the door, there is one more ceremony of farewell which takes place between us—so regularly it has become a ritual. Just before you disappear down the stairway you look back and up, and I am waiting for that look; our eyes meet, and in that contact you assert, and I acknowledge, a secret bond. It is secret because you do not choose to express it. It seems to you more secure, I think, if it is not entrusted to words. But yesterday it was not secure, it was threatened by the intrusion. And that must have made you feel that the bond is fragile or illusory, that it may be lost."

The next day she was light in manner, affectionate. Just at the end of the hour, however, she began to stammer, looked at her watch, cleared her throat. "Before I leave . . . I wanted to say . . ." She hesitated, corrected herself, "I *want* to say . . . I love you very much."

Dr. Melville understands that she is grateful. She has never mentioned having thrown herself at him, he knows she never will. But he senses she is grateful he did not accept, that he does not despise her for it, that he does not remind her of it, that he permits it to be a secret memory between them.

Sometimes there wells up in her gaze something more, he thinks, than gratitude. But that thought places him before a door which opens upon ungovernable desire. It would sweep them away. He went that way before, will not do so again. He knows what would happen. Then he was unready, now he would not turn back. But now he loves her more truly; it is for her sake he will not go back to that edge and plunge with her. He tries to preclude the possibility, to lock the door, to throw away the key; reminds himself that whereas he, looking back to her, finds the twenty-eight years between them to be no gulf at all, no barrier to the most intimate of touching, of mingling, she, from the other side of those same years, looks across a vast gulf, sees an old man. So old indeed that she can say, "I love you very much," with the immunity of a daughter. Remember that, he warns himself. Do not mislead her a second time.

She has met a young violinist from the New York Philharmonic Orchestra, here on vacation. They are playing through the Beethoven and Schubert sonatas.

CORA has virtually disappeared from Dr. Melville's life. Her manner is cool, has a quality also of shrewdness, of calculation. For some weeks she has been sleeping in the guest room. Dr. Melville has been so immersed in longing for Lori he has hardly noticed. Now that he thinks of it he realizes she is preparing to divorce him. He recalls having seen in the mail recently certain memoranda from banks, from lawyers and accountants, as would suggest that their estate is being prepared for division. Must mean her affair is going well. Also that her lover is well heeled. He doesn't care. It seems remote, unimportant. There is nothing left between them, he wishes her well. He has been a meal-ticket for her; she doesn't need that any longer. She has been for him a shield, and he doesn't need that any longer. His attachment to Lori, the depths between them, exposes the shallowness of the bargain he and Cora struck so long ago.

But that's unfair, he thinks. We lost it, that's all. If it now seems shallow, so one day may this love for Lori. He reads old love letters. Compact of hopes that could never have been realized but which seemed so possible. The greatness of expectations, the hope, the passion . . . scaled down, compromised, given up, and what was left, so soon, the merest shadow of what seemed then in prospect.

But might it not be, he thinks, that the pursuit of that illusion is grander, more to be desired, than the plain view? What if I were starting out again? Would I want from the outset to see it as illusory, and so feel none of that wild and wrenching passion, and hence none of the pain? Or would I want to feel again as I felt then? As I feel now, for Lori?

What I'm wanting to escape from, he thinks, is nothing other than normal everyday life. I am, by almost any standard, exceedingly fortunate. Could even get Cora back if I wanted, if I tried, if I cared. Few are so lucky. Yet I can hardly bear this normal, this fortunate life, and so am driving myself into a frenzy of unrequited and unrequitable love. As an escape. Romantic love is made for despair. That's the whole point. It is a rejection of that happiness of which, with a bit of resignation, we might be capable, in favor of a despair which will properly register our protest against the loss of Eden.

THIS longing, he thinks, measures a lost oneness. The wound is covered over, with the salves and ointments of whatever relationships one can manage, but never heals. Certain faces evoke that primal wholeness, suggest it can be regained, that it's possible, that with luck it might just happen. The dagger of longing slithers through one's heart. But they are lost, these faces. They smile with that hint of promise, then disappear down that hall, that stairway, into elevators, airplanes, are lost in crowds—and the pain of that first severence comes back, sharp as ever, the wound is open, never heals.

CORA is away. Dr. Melville paces about the house, one end to the other, around and around, baffled, trying to find the bars to his cage. He is in an anguish of longing, is agitated, drives to Telegraph Hill, across the bridge to Marin, back to Telegraph Hill. At night he sits in his office, lights out, a pain in his heart he cannot fling aside. Sometimes he speaks aloud. This will pass, he tells himself. It will. It must. Just hold still, it will pass. During the mornings he watches the clock, lives for two-thirty, for that moment their eyes will meet as she comes up the stairs, for that shy inward smile which both exalts and torments his feverish soul. As she lies on the couch he leans over in his chair, hand alive with the impulse to touch her hair, aware of every breath she takes, of the slightest movement of her strong slender hands, her slim extended body. The minutes fly by. They are gone. Then that moment of parting, of drowning once more in those dark pools, that last look from the stairs, back and up, eyes meeting, reaffirming the secret bond. And afterward . . . replaying all she has said . . . then the long afternoon with other patients, oh and night, sitting in the dark, staring, waiting out the hours, the minutes, till the next day when he will see her again.

THIS longing, he knows, betrays the modestly good life that would otherwise be possible for the sake of a transcendent life not possible on earth, replaces simple pleasures at hand with an anguished yearning for some great good forever out of reach.

Take heed, he warns himself. One day, a day lying in wait up ahead, you will lie abed in a hospital, writhe in nausea from chemotherapy, feel the metastases spreading out in your bones, hair falling in bunches from the radiation—and what then will seem to you to have been the way to live? Does the dark-haired beauty still beckon? Do you strain to follow, to reach out, to touch? Or do you yearn rather but to walk on the beach in the sun, to sit down to dinner with a friend, or perhaps just to be free of pain—all those riches which are now right at hand and ignored?

HER violinist, she tells Dr. Melville, has been in a vile mood. They have a fight, for three days do not speak. Then, slowly, they begin to talk. He is nice to her. They talk for hours. They go to bed, hold each other, continue to talk. Talking becomes murmuring. "Hold me tighter," she says. She kisses his ear, wet with her tears, feels herself opening. "I love you so much," she says. "I love you," he says.

Over and over, his heart breaking, Dr. Melville plays this scene.

I'm such a fool, he thinks. Psychoanalyst mooning over his young patient. Dotty old professor trotting after the Blue Angel. I astonish myself. Why do I permit such indignity? Why don't I analyze it away?

SHE comes four days a week, Monday through Thursday. When she leaves on Thursday he is desolate: three full days before he will see her. He doesn't like that "three," tries not to think of it, will think of it tomorrow when it will have become "two." On Friday it's a little better, but two is still an eternity. But tomorrow, he consoles himself, I will be able to say "day after tomorrow." On Sunday his spirits rise: tomorrow I will see her. As I lie dying, he thinks, my regret will be to leave a world in which still she lives and moves, in which, therefore I might still see and touch her.

Like a knife in his heart is that missed opportunity, the scene always present behind his eyes: she stands before him, arms outstretched, wearing that ridiculous dress, taking the big chance, offering herself. Her anguished voice rings in his ears; "Don't you *want* me?" He cannot forgive himself. Of course it was impermissible. Of course it could not last. Of course it would have destroyed him. He corrects himself—*might* have destroyed him. He knows analysts who have survived such things. Of course it would have been unfair to her. All true. All true. Still he should have done it. There are occasions for which not reason, nor principle, nor morality, is a guide. That was such a moment. Against all he knew to be right he should have followed his heart, should have accepted. Should have taken her in his arms, gratefully. And then should have loved her so deeply, so creatively, as to have found a way to redeem that violation of limits which, in ordinary circumstances, should never be violated. That is what he should have done. Not to fall helplessly, but to leap with her from that precipice. Maybe they could have learned to fly.

What followed thereafter seems to validate his remorse. She could not have long remained on that knife edge, was going to fall, either to him or to Charles. Better to him. Far better. For whereas Amelia was shattered, was almost destroyed, it would hardly have shaken Cora, would have but emboldened her to a more daring course. Too late. Too late. He writhes in pain, cannot forgive himself.

HE could, perhaps, dispel this longing, invoke a vision of himself and of Lori which would bathe them in the drab light of everyday, render them flawed, replaceable, such that either one could walk away with but a nod. She is a siren, but her seductiveness does not work with every man; it works with him only because of something in him reciprocal to her vulnerability. Most likely that dreaded, that insecurely warded-off self-image: the weakling. In every shadow lurks the beast. At any moment— who knows when?—through that blue door, from behind that bush, under that stone or leaf, at any crossroad, it may spring. Will he stand and fight, or will he cringe?

Will his lips remain sealed under torture, or will he name names? Lori's shy vulnerability makes him feel like St. George with mailed foot on slain dragon. Of course he loves her. His love has a secret agenda. He is trying to cure some wounded and rejected part of self.

Now there's an insight, he thinks. A tool. Use it with vigor and scorn, and this infatuation will vanish. . . . Perhaps. The tool lies inert in the workshop of his mind. He picks it up, fingers it, considers what it could do with will and muscle behind it, then drops it. He cannot bring himself to dismantle this infatuation. Allegiance to reality, he thinks, is acceptance of death. He chooses illusion over reality.

LOOKING through the attic, through old trunks and boxes, Dr. Melville comes upon a ghost from his adolescence. A large print, glass-covered, narrow gilt frame. "Penny a Bunch"—shows a child offering violets for sale. The picture is sentimental, the appeal is meretricious; he is appalled, also curious, that he had, even as a boy, allowed it to touch him so deeply. That was forty years ago, he has not thought of it since, yet it all comes tumbling back. The first time a picture had meant anything to him. It stood on an easel in the window of an art supplies store. He does not remember the price, perhaps five or ten dollars, a fortune to him. He stood before the window, looked, took it into his soul; and again and again whenever he could he came back to look. Seeing the picture, he now remembers the day, the moment, sees also himself outside the store window looking in—awkward, isolated, sure that no one could ever love him.

The center of the picture is the face of the child, a skinny somewhat boyish girl of six or seven years; toward the periphery everything fades to an impressionistic blur, though one can make out that she stands in a city street. She is in rags, barefoot, her abundant chestnut hair in a wild tangle. Around her neck is a strap supporting a shallow flat basket which she holds at waist level containing several bunches of violets. Her head is turned sharply to the right, looking back and up; someone has just caught her attention, startling her. Her left hand steadies the basket, her right hand, extended, offers a bunch of violets. Tentatively, diffidently, ready to turn away if rejected. The large wide-open eyes, frightened and beseeching, reflect the color of her violets.

Instantly he had known her, filled in her personality, her circumstances, become her protector. The passionate, spiritual face bespoke a depth of awareness born of suffering, the need to be loved and the capacity to love. It was clear to him that she lived outside the pale of those experiences of which she was capable, for which she was meant. She was a princess of spirit, but had been so kicked about that she had lost knowledge of her royal birth, thought of herself as a ragamuffin. Her story had come to him complete, instantly, as if it were his own. She was the only child of a drunken father who beat her and a wanton mother who neglected her. Tormented by their abuse, she did their bidding, gave over to them the pennies she earned, cringed at their blows, ate her crust of bread in the corner, slept huddled on the floor by the stove. And in the mornings would go out in the woods to pick her violets, would tie them into bunches with dry grass, sell them in the city for her shiftless parents. But she was nevertheless a princess, and he felt somehow himself ennobled to have recognized her fineness.

She had won his heart, became his icon. He kept coming back to look until he had saved enough money to buy, then saved for months more to have her suitably framed. She then hung on his wall and lived in his heart. He was hooked by her shyness, wanted to rescue her from her sense of unworthiness. It became his crusade, his entrancement. What tempted him in her, what continues to tempt him in her successors, what sweeps him away, is the prospect that his love of her may enable her to think well of herself.

So that's the way it is, he thinks. She is no *other*, she is I. In loving her I love myself, in rescuing her I redeem a part of myself—weak, frightened, feminine—of which otherwise I must be ashamed. Here in this attic I have found an idealized portrait of my hidden self, just as I found it in that store window so long ago, as I have found it in all those other shy dark beauties in between. This is the secret of all that swooning: it is not *they* whom I have loved; they have been but the gilt frames within which I have discovered and swooned over—myself. My lovelorn enslavement is to a lurking image in a dark mirror. And the color of those violets reflected in the frightened eyes of this child, is the very same as that which now, forty years later, has found its way into the eyes of my patient, who looks at me from the stairs, looks back and up in the same movement, the same posture, of this long-forgotten flower girl.

HE remembers Marlene. There was violet, surely, in her dark eyes. He met her one evening at the home of a friend. A long time ago. Her husband dominated the conversation, smart, maybe a bit smart-ass, anyway a lot to say, rather loud and funny. She was quiet and serious. Fair skin, oval face, large blue-violet eyes with dark lashes and dark brows. Her hair was gold with streaks of dark, long and glistening, drawn back straight with a clasp from which it hung down loose to her waist. Her face was dominated by the enormous eyes. They sucked up the world, devoured it (she wanted to be a writer), but in appearance they seemed rather to expose *her* to the world's hunger, creating a vulnerability which made him instantly protective. He thought her husband didn't deserve her. Anyway, those eyes watched him intently. He had recently had some success, an article on psychoanalysis in *The Atlantic*, and she was perhaps envious. Also she liked him. Anyway, she asked questions, seemed to want to be with him. When they said goodnight their hands clasped firmly, their eyes met, held, they were aware of attraction. Aware also of being in control. They sensed what might have been, what still could be if they should be swept away. But she was a young mother, he was but recently married, the time was not right. They were not swept away. They said goodnight and parted and he did not telephone her, but thought of her, felt her eyes on him, knew she was thinking of him. They had moved through a pivotal moment, wavered on a knife-edge, and decided on discretion.

These things happen, one survives. He would have forgotten it, was on his way to forgetting, when there occurred a second and more crucial moment, a more anguished wavering, followed by the same decision. The corner where it happened haunts him still. Clay and Locust. Twenty-five years, and still he feels a pang on passing. Like a grave. A whole life that might might have been, a life like any other with its special qualities of passion, conflict, sicknesses, children, troubles, travels— all that lies buried at that corner. No stone to mark the place, but he knows; he remembers the snap of steel on flint, the spark they didn't shield with their hands, didn't blow on, that went out.

What happened? Such a little thing, he can say it in a sentence: She was driving, he was walking, they waved, she passed on. That's it. Took about three seconds. But he has run the loop of those three seconds before his remorseful soul hour after hour, day after day, for all those years, has blown up the film until her gesture is lost in graininess, diminished it again, with no loosening of its grip on him. There is no way to look at it or analyze it that will dispel the pain. He can believe a face could launch a thousand ships, it could if he were king. It did not on that morning, and he is racked still by an expedition to Troy he did not make.

He remembers more. It was a few weeks after they had met, about eight o'clock of a weekday morning. Monday, he thinks. He had walked the dog, was returning home. She had, he surmises, taken her son to nursery school. She came round the corner from Clay Street onto Locust. They saw each other at the same moment, smiled, waved; the car slowed, faltered, went on. That's all. That's the loop. He slows it down, runs it through again. He saw

her first, recognized her first—this despite the fact that
he was in the open, in full view, on the sidewalk, whereas
she was inside a moving car behind a reflecting wind-
shield. He infers from this that she had perhaps been
more vividly and constantly in his thoughts for those last
weeks than he in hers. She had that tense manner and
dishevelled appearance of a housewife on Monday morning. No makeup, had not brushed her hair, perhaps not
even washed her face. She had been up late, at a party,
he chose to imagine, got to bed about two, submitted
agreeably but with minimal responsiveness to the horni-
ness of her talkative husband. In the morning, having
overslept, she rushed to get her son dressed and fed, threw
off her nightgown, pulled a dress over her naked body,
pushed her bare feet into slippers, and drove him off to
school. So there she was, harrassed, smelling faintly of
sperm, taking the corner a little too fast, and sees a man
waving at her. Then she recognized him and waved. They
were smiling at each other. The car slowed a bit because,
as he reconstructs it, she lifted her foot from the accelerator, creating a pause for their greeting, and in that pause,
that thousandth of a second, the contact between them
deepened, regained that intense attraction, that awareness of possibility. What an explosive vision, that car
careening around the corner, that carriage with a golden
princess! He had conjured her from desire, his preoccu-
pation and fantasies had invoked her; and so perhaps there
was in his smile something of special gladness and triumph,
omnipotence. Then came that faltering of the car upon
which his heart too has faltered over the years. He knows
what happened, what must have happened. The motion

of the car, which was slowing because she had lifted her foot from the accelerator, faltered because that foot now touched the brake. That was the crucial, the pivotal moment, because that added hesitation unmistakably signalled a willingness to receive his advance. Even in all her rush and surprise and dishabillé, those great blue eyes were smiling and wet and open to him, and that foot which he could not see was touching the brake, creating that lapse, that lurch of motion, like the stutter in a declaration of illicit love—that was the moment! That was the receptivity into which he could have flung himself headlong, the vortex that would have swallowed up all his pain. He had only to raise his arms, call her name, anything. She would have stopped. And then and there in the midst of all that unlikeliness would have begun that whole new life with its unforeseeable consequences stretching endlessly ahead. But he didn't raise his arms, did not call her name, just smiled, and a lifetime was lost. A delicate foot that he could not see, a foot with a faint down of blonde hair (in a worn-down bedroom slipper), left the brake it had touched so lightly, went back to the accelerator, and the instant of faltering ended in a smooth forward motion. And he would never be the same again.

"WE were walking on a mountain path," Lori said. "You and I. All around us were high peaks covered with ice and snow. No wind, no sound. Very cold. The path was rocky and bare. I was leading, running on ahead, I was happy. We were going north. On and on we went, for days. The mountains got higher. More and more ice. Then the path opened up on the left. We came to the edge of a cliff, the rock fell away, we could look straight down a great distance, perhaps miles, to a deep blue sea. Too high to hear the surf. Everything was completely still. It was very beautiful. As we stood there I became aware of something strange in the water, bands of a slightly darker blue. They were curved. Concentric arcs, as in a rainbow. Not easy to see, but definite. Something in the water, maybe currents of algae, being oriented in one direction, perhaps by magnetism. Then I realized—it came suddenly like an inspiration—that the center of the circle defined by those arcs was exactly where we were standing. I felt great happiness, exaltation. It was the end of our journey. I took your arm. 'Look! Look! We must be standing at the north pole.' And you looked and saw what I saw. And we stood there, filled with wonder, seeming to grow taller in our happiness. And it seemed to me then that the world was a potter's wheel, and that at that moment we were the bit of clay at the center, we were being shaped, and I leaned back and stretched my arms up over my head, higher and higher, and felt myself being created by some force, by whatever was making those blue circles in the water. I was so happy!"

DR. MELVILLE remembers the ending of *Children of Paradise*. The mime pushing through the crowd, calling, calling, "Garance! Garance!" People dancing in the streets, celebrating, jostling, the crowd becoming more packed, impenetrable, like a wall, the mime struggling, Garance disappearing, his cry more anguished, despairing, "Gaa-*rance!*" One's heart breaks. He remembers Lara driving off in the sleigh with Komarovsky, believing Zhivago will follow. The frozen fields, the last glow of setting sun, the snow already purple in the hollows, the wolves; Zhivago watching for the last glimpse of the sleigh as it flashes into sight across the ravine, then disappears. "We shall not meet again in this life, farewell, my love, my inexhaustible, everlasting joy." It pulls one apart. Everything shouts a protest.

But what a curious thing! To weep for the loss of something admittedly an illusion. Nothing warrants it, nothing supports it. It is not of this world. All we know about love denies it—in spades. We know what happens when Garance hears that anguished cry and goes back, when Lara leaps from the sleigh and slogs back through the darkening drifts to Varykino. They get married and love dies. That's what happens. They get on each other's nerves, they fight, wound each other, make up; they fall into deepening resentments, contempt, bitterness, hostility; they withdraw from each other, arrive at some position of wary guardedness, of armed and disappointed truce; and finally, if they're lucky, they stake out some little corner of shared life where they can be friendly, fond of each other. That's what love is. What it comes to be. The tragedy is not that we die but that we do not die of love, we turn away, forget, rush headlong into forgetting, into everydayness until, of that high moment, finally, nothing remains. So whence this belief that what might have been is something exalted, transcendent? Surely, for any pair of lovers, the accident of their being lost to each other cannot in itself create the possibility that *their* love, given a chance, would escape the general fate. Dr. Melville knows what would happen to him and Lori. Yet the belief is ineluctable. It is as though it had been *promised*. And we hold on to that promise in the face of all we know, in the face of the entire accumulated experience of mankind.

We won't give it up. We carry it about like a claim-check to a state of bliss. Getting ever more soiled and dog-eared, that claim-check remains our most treasured possession. Like a drunk applying for a job with his ancient and tattered letter of recommendation, we're always hauling it out of our pocket and presenting it, hoping to establish credibility. We present it to one woman after another throughout our lives, always disappointed, always explaining away our disappointment—it was the wrong woman, maybe the next time . . .

LORI'S violinist friend has gone back to New York; the symphony season has begun. They talk often on the phone. He is coming back for a weekend next month. She talks a lot about Juillard, a teacher there she would like to work with.

One day at the door, as she was leaving, she reached out her hand—was it, Dr. Melville wonders, the right or the left? The right, he thinks. Yes, he is sure. The fingers trembled. They touched his sleeve, so lightly as barely to be felt, like a butterfly. The two of them stood there for a moment talking—something about a change of schedule next week—looking at each other, very close, unaware of the danger. Or rather *she* was unaware. Dr. Melville felt himself spinning, knew he was approaching that precipice again. She wore a navy blue dress. Very elegant. Something she had put on, he felt sure, just for him. There was a bit of old lace at her throat. And all her wonderful womanliness. Dark. Radiant. Glorious. Then she was gone.

She is preparing to say good-by. He knows it. Has been dreading it. This was the first clear intimation. A few weeks, a few months at most, and she will be going down those stairs for the last time.

She would like, she says, to give him back gratitude equal to the help he has given her. He notes his disappointment. It is not gratitude he wants, but love. Gratitude wants nothing. He wants her to want something of him; for only so may he want something of her, and only that mutual wanting could bind them together. Not the friendly embrace which loosens on the moment, but a deep clenching that will not let go.

He is caught up in a savage and mournful yearning. Caught, held, transfixed, pointed in one direction. Still trying to reason his way through it, to figure it out—an iron filing in a magnetic field trying to formulate the laws of magnetism. His heart is breaking. He cannot recall his projections, can no longer even recognize them. The pain is so intense he cannot work, cannot read.

ON impulse she flies to New York for a weekend. Dr. Melville drives to Telegraph Hill, walks about her house, looking, feeling himself into it, putting himself in her place, seeing what she sees: the carport where she parks, the pile of wood for the fireplace, the door she enters, the back steps down which she carries the garbage, the high windows from which she looks out. He strains to enter, to float through her rooms. He knows her so well, knows what she will never tell another, yet still is a beggar (or a thief!), holds her so slightly, possesses but a bit of her, yearns for the whole. When he gathers up in his two hands all of her that she has given him, it seems so little, hardly any weight at all. He wants more, wants to enter, to sit at the piano, touch the keys her fingers touch, look at the lines of music her eyes follow, the pictures on her walls, the view of the bay which greets her in the mornings; wants to sit at her desk, look at the letters she has received, the rough drafts perhaps of letters she has written, bills to be paid, notes to herself, photographs of her family; wants to see the books on her shelves, and the books she currently is reading which stand in a pile by her chair; would enter the bathroom, sniff the soaps and lotions which touch her skin, would find the scent he knows from his own stairway as she mounts to him, would look at the toothbrush which scrubs her teeth; even the stool, that humble throne of creatureliness, being hers, would be dear to him; and somewhere he would find her diaphragm, would touch it, hold it to his face, kiss it, straining for closeness to that depth of her known to this murky disc; (but no—it strikes his heart like a dagger!— he would not find it, the diaphragm is with her in New York); in her bedroom he would open her closet, would recognize dresses, blouses, pants, shoes—old friends!— would see others strange to him suggesting experiences of which he knows nothing, would open drawers wherein everything would be strange—bras, slips, underpants— and many of these, he would think, perhaps all of them, have been in my office though never till now have I seen them; would lie on her bed beside that place where he would imagine her ordinarily to lie, would put his arms around that emptiness, draw it close to him.

He yearns to be inside, to do all these things, to make other discoveries he cannot now imagine. He would do no harm, would disturb nothing, would touch most lightly, would hover as a loving and guardian angel among her things.

That's a lie, he thinks, I would not be so gentle, so hovering, so harmless, I want to devour her utterly, and even this violation of her house, however bountiful its harvest of secrets, of intimacies, would not be enough, I still would not *know* her. Indeed it would be but symbolic of that more radical looking and possessing for which he really hungers. He wants in sacred, perhaps cannibalistic ritual, to unwrap her, piece by piece, until she stands before him in glorious nakedness and womanliness, wants then to enter her most deeply, stir slumbrous flesh to tumult, to wave upon crashing wave, till finally they, both of them, lie spent and beached upon some far shore of mournful victory. And even that distant place, so far far beyond where he could ever hope to go with her in fact, even that, he knows, would not be far enough, and he would lie beside her, passion-flung on that remote shore, as far as ever from his elusive goal, knowing then no way to press on further.

So soon, he thinks, as we become aware of the gulf which separates our severed and mortal state from that wholeness to which our very bones make claim, at that moment the longing begins . . . and from that moment forward it continues . . . flinging itself headlong, recklessly, at one woman after another, at those faces which hold promise of that wholeness and so snatch up that longing . . . and so it goes . . . on and on and on till the day we die.

MEDITATION

. . . hell is made up of yearnings. The wicked
don't roast on beds of nails, they sit on comfortable chairs and are tortured with yearnings.

ISAAC BASHEVIS SINGER

X ~~~ o

Desire

WERE I well adjusted this book would not have been written. The semblance is intact, suggests poise, adjustment, knowing how, but I'm inside, I know what I know. No one becomes a psychoanalyst without worms gnawing at his soul.

EARLY in the morning I arrive at my immaculate airy office, open the French doors, sink into my chair, pick up my writing of yesterday . . . put it aside, watch the wind billow the lace curtains. Misery fills my soul, much as the cool gray light wells up and fills the room. It is inadmissible. If I speak of it to my wife, she protests, reminds me how fortunate I am, of the many who live in want, in danger, in bondage. All true. And every such consideration increases my shame. If I persist, she becomes resentful, says I am dragging her down. And she's right.

Such despair, in the midst of ease, of affluence, is disloyalty to life. There is something disgusting about it, a fouling of the pool of life in which all are immersed.

I could perhaps deny it, but cannot give it up. It is what I am. Inalienable. I think of the day ahead, the patients I will see, their special varieties of trouble, of uncertainty, of suffering. With them I have a quite special obligation to embody the possibility of arriving at an adjustment which permits the affirmation of life. The adjustments I do in fact help them achieve—usually with more denial than is possible for me—provide them with more basis for such affirmation than I can find within myself.

So here I am, an incontinent man, swimming around with loved ones, friends, patients, in the pool of life, treading water, paddling about, chatting, laughing, commenting on the weather like everybody else. If I tell them I am fouling the water I spoil the fun for everyone. If I keep quiet and pretend all is well I am in bad faith.

WE analysts are very defensive about our theory. As well we might be. Conjectural excess has always been our method. "It may be surmised that . . ." "We may assume that . . ." "It seems possible that . . ." These phrases thread their way through our literature, in and out, modest little bridges between clinical finding and some new proposition designed to explain that finding, the proposition always advanced as a "hypothesis," thereby claiming scientific status, yet always non-verifiable and non-falsifiable. It comes about finally that simply the showing of clinical data as *consonant* with the hypothesis is taken as proof of the hypothesis.

As conjectures acquire credibility by such use, and become venerable also with age, with mere survival, insidiously they cease to be hypotheses and come to be facts—upon which new conjectures may then be built. And every one of us wants to do a little building. We get out our little hammers—master builders every one of us!—and tack on some new bit of gingerbread to an already overloaded, already dangerously overhanging, already too baroque balcony. Our theory is now a Winchester House, that mystery house of a thousand rooms, secret doors and passageways, different levels, always changing, crazy angles, one room connecting obscurely with the next, the whole thing the product of its owner's belief (Winchester's widow, I think) that so long as the house was unfinished she would not die—*that* hypothesis having been advanced by her palmist. That's what our theory is like, and it's quite understandable we might be defensive about it.

But there's something else we assume, more basic, more important, about which we're not defensive at all. Indeed we seem unaware of it, take it so for granted, like the air we breathe, so self-evidently true that its truth need no longer be remarked. That assumption is simply that it is possible for a human being to be well adjusted, to have a good life, that however rare it may be in fact it is in principle possible. There are a few psychoanalytic asides, always jocose, which stand as disclaimers. "Analysis enables you to cope with the misery of real life," or "to adjust to the poverty in which it leaves you." But this is window-dressing, a specious cynicism to ward off the embarrassment of a real utopianism. The assumption is basic and ubiquitous. Without it we'd have to pack up our couch and ottoman and fade away. Our so-called science is married to a genuine faith: that serious and sustained misery is not inherent to human life, that it is imposed by neurotic conflict or by reality hardship; that, therefore, if neurotic conflict is analyzed and resolved and if reality hardship is absent one will love and will work, will live out one's span with contentment, with real gratifications, and when the end comes will pronounce it all to have been worth while.

Of course, we say, there is always reality hardship, and that's true. But no, not *always*. For it's also true—rather blatantly, even embarrassingly, true—that many of us in America, most particularly those of us who can afford psychoanalysis, are often free of reality hardship, are in good health, have money, are well married, have suffered no loss. Are we well adjusted? Are analysts well adjusted? As a group we are spectacularly free of reality hardship, and are very well analyzed. What would I say of my own life? Of the lives of my colleagues?

We are deceived, and we have deceived others. The good life is possible when awareness is limited, but it is not possible for us. We know too much. Were we to know only the world we'd be all right. But knowledge spills over. We know also ourselves, our destructiveness, our hunger for immortality, our oncoming death. Our knowledge subverts adjustment at the root. The misery inheres in what we are. The ideal is incoherent.

In the afternoons I see patients, in the mornings I write. Helping others is ephemeral, writing is my real work. Or so I have thought. Over the years I have published six long papers on the structural theory of psychoanalysis, but now this work has slowed. More and more I merely sit in my office in the mornings watching the lace curtains billow in and out, hearing the traffic sounds from Bush Street, staring at the wall. I have become aware that I have been straining to write in stone, to create a theory that would displace others, install itself as the canon of psychoanalysis. My disaffection is not that I have failed— I have the energy and the will to go on—but that the goal was illusory. My work has established itself, is much referred to, but I feel scornful. Nothing can be falsified in psychoanalysis. Kohut cannot displace Hartmann. Freud wanted to be, not only right, but right in such a way as would prove others wrong. In this he fails. We all fail. Freud makes his appeal—and a very powerful appeal it is—not by being preemptively right about anything, but by offering a vision of human life that makes sense of our experience. But it doesn't make complete sense, nor exclusive sense. No one is drummed out, no view is exorcized. Jung makes his appeal in the same way. And Rank and Sullivan and Horney and all the rest. A chorus of contending voices, each with a catchy tune, and each claiming to be the one true theme. How we are to make sense of our lives is not something that some great genius can get straight once and for all, but an ongoing task of interpretation in a changing field.

Earlier in my life I chafed at clinical work, would have preferred to be a full-time investigator and writer. As I have grown older, however, and have become aware of how shabby, tattered, and unread are most of those messages nailed against the wall of eternity, I have begun to feel fortunate in my work with patients, honored at being trusted with secrets which entail so much vulnerability, grateful at being able to help.

The bad thing about being old is knowing so much, which makes it impossible to learn anything new. The too experienced eye cannot see the world afresh, has seen too much already, knows there's nothing new, sees only what it already knows to be there. So one is left behind with his wisdom; the static vision becomes stale while, unnoticed, the world turns, becomes something new.

Oh to be young again, awash in inexperience, everything to be encountered, grasped, understood, for the first time! How reclaim that seminal ignorance? How give up being the old pro?

LONG line at the bank. Four tellers. This will take about ten minutes, I estimate. Take my place at the end of the line, begin reading my newspaper. I move forward, one or two steps at a time, newcomers fall into place behind me. One of the tellers, I observe, is a trainee; an experienced teller sits beside her, supervising. Avoid her, I tell myself, she will take forever. I look at my watch, am nearing the head of the line, will pass up my turn if it is she who becomes available to me. Yet my gaze is locked on her. She wears a sleeveless sweater of muted colors over a white blouse; dusky skin; holds herself quite erect, an air of dignity. A supple neck, like the curving stem of a tulip, extends upward from the white collar, blossoms into . . . no, not blossoms, not yet, she's too young. Buds, rather, a dark tulip bud. Full lips, slender nose, large eyes. I am at the head of the line now, the supervisor points out something to her, she smiles, is grateful for instruction. Her manner is both warm and shy. Her customer nods and leaves. She looks up at me. And at the same moment the teller beyond her is also free, calls out "Next!" I walk forward quickly, can now pass her by without implication of rejection, yet am stopped abruptly, as by a brick wall, impulse subverting intention. I stand before her, breathing fast.

"How is it going for you?" I ask, sliding forward some checks to be deposited. Large eyes set widely apart, a rather dark blue. Long curving eyelashes. Reserve, restraint, great dignity. A waif, but like the daughter of a king. Her hair is dark, falls below her shoulders. "Oh, *very* well," she says, grateful for my good will with its promise of patience with her inexperience. Correct pronunciation but definite accent. The three words hang in the air like musical notes, quiver, dazzle me. She begins checking over the deposit slip. "Is this your first day?" "Oh no," she says, "I'm starting my second week." Again that musical reverberation. Her words touch me like fingers, light, cool, caressing, Exotic accent. My mouth is dry. "Are you Scandinavian?" "No . . ." she hesitates, a slight faltering, "Persian."

Persian? Ah, Iranian. An exile from home, an enemy here. "Persian" is a plea, means, "Do not condemn me. It is not I who held your hostages." Poor kid. Probably has no money; the blouse is inexpensive, the sweater handknit. The supervisor is pointing out something to her. She listens seriously, conscientiously, wants to learn, feels lucky to have found this job. Suddenly I am ashamed of the large sum I am depositing. She probably has nothing. Slender waist, wears dark pants. She is giving me a receipt. "Thank you," she says. My business with her is over, I can find no reason to stay. "I hope it goes well for you here," I say. "Oh, thank you." She blushes.

I walk away, out of the building, dizzy, reeling. I sit in my car, staring, do not turn on the ignition, have forgotten my rush, where I was going, the pressure of time. A pain spreads out in me as if I would die. I try to argue it away. Bring back her face. Fragile, vulnerable, poised. Beautiful, to be sure, but why am I so affected? What about her breasts? Did I notice? Can't remember. Probably small. Something slim and boyish about her. And so young. Iranian is a bad word; of course she's Persian. Something terribly decent in the way she said it, with but the slightest hesitation; wants to disclaim connection with the Khomeini tyranny, yet not deny her origin.

I move my head from side to side in a torment of longing. Try to shake it away. Why such desperation? She is indeed beautiful, but some beautiful faces leave me unmoved. Is it that pliant vulnerability, that hint of receptivity, that she might yield to my intention, be shaped by my will, a Galatea waiting in marble for my chisel? My urgent, throbbing chisel! Words! Words! That exotic face, that slim form, have entered my heart, set me afire. I start the car, roar away as if to have done with her, to leave her behind. To no avail. She has knifed into my heart. She goes with me.

WHAT causes the world to have meaning? And what causes that meaning to drain away? What leads us to be attached to the world, and what causes those attachments to falter? Like the water table beneath a flourishing land, sex nourishes the life above it. From it derive not only fields of wheat, tall trees, green meadows, but also the play of children, the sound of axe and saw. When it drains away, the life above it dries up, withers, is gone with the wind.

I COME from a line of elongated consumptives, and as a child seemed likely to continue the strain; you could count every rib. My grandmother encircled my skinny arm with worn fingers, regarded me sadly. "Son, you must eat. You must put some flesh on those bones."

I heard a lot about this need for flesh on my bones. And a lot, also, about flesh in a different context. Throughout my childhood I sat on the rough benches of country churches in the South and stared up spellbound at a black storm of a preacher thundering about the sins of the flesh, the evil and the temptation of the flesh, the treacherous enticements of the flesh which would sweep one away from God's grace into eternal hellfire. I believed but was mystified, and at home alone would flex my arm, observe the growing muscle, touch it, puzzled, unable to find in this flesh, which my grandmother said I should have more of, either dire evil or forbidden pleasure.

But some years later, as I lay abed of a spring night, the warm air drifting heavy with honeysuckle through the open window over my exposed body, my swollen member took on a life of its own, was taken over, rather, by a current of life which I thenceforth would bear forward as carrier rather than master, and in that current, as I at once realized, was both the pleasure and the evil of which I had been warned.

IN the bookstore the paperback fiction is arranged alphabetically by author. After Sherwood Anderson comes Anonymous, that great master of erotica. *The Boudoir, A Man With A Maid, My Secret Life.* (Jane Austen, on the other side, shrinks back, offended.) All of the great works of literature are arrayed there before me, from Agee to Zola, all available for uplift of soul, but I stand rooted before that hypnotic master Anonymous. I take a volume from the shelf. It's not difficult to find a detailed, explicit passage. I read to the end, two or three pages at most, return the book to the shelf, take out another. I handle the books with care, intent not to soil a cover or crease a page; for I will not buy, would not own such a book, take it home, no more than a heroin addict, trying to stop, would have a supply of drug in the house. I am yielding to a vice, but only for a moment, will not surrender to it. To possess such a book, read it leisurely, start to finish, leave it on my night table, shelve it in my bookcase— that fullness of violation is beyond me. Mine is a hit-and-run encounter. I read quickly, one or two passages, hold the book apprehensively, guiltily, know myself to be in bad faith; for I am not really above this stuff as I would like to think, nor am I an honest customer. I am a pretender. I am making an unauthorized loan—am a thief of lust!—therefore feel barely tolerated here, increasingly sensitive to the comings and goings of clerks, suspect that each one as he passes identifies the passage being read. I shrink back against the shelves, try not to block the passageway. My mouth becomes dry, I have reached my limit. I replace the book, move on. To diffuse the specificity of my interest I pause in brief dissimulation before Moravia and Updike, then leave the store.

I turn west up Clement Street into the wind. There is a metallic taste in my mouth, a weak and empty feeling in my stomach. This isn't it. I feel soiled and corrupt. I am further away from it now than before. Life is a treasure hunt. I have to play, there isn't anything else, but I am being given mischievous clues: "Find a pearl in the outhouse."

AT my dentist's office, a woman in the waiting room. Had been brushing her hair, stopped as the door opened. She now replaces brush and mirror in her handbag, opens a magazine. She is sitting by a table lamp, her hair luminous in the glow. I sit in a corner, unobtrusively to observe her. She is very beautiful. I begin to feel the familiar pain. And she is young enough, I think mournfully, to be my daughter. No, the other way round: I am old enough to be her father; for I would not want her any less young. Slender and—I take the measure of her long legs—tall. The legs are stockinged and crossed, high heels. Silk dress, mauve. Why so dressed up? Maybe a first visit. Her hair is dark, silky, a disarray of planned abandon. Her face is not happy, not serene, but has a noble perfection of line, a natural reserve and dignity—and a latent turbulence, something somber, brooding, passionate. She feels me looking at her, glances up with a frown. I am in a storm of exaltation and despair. Here I am again, I think wildly, at the same old place: the gates of heaven, without key or password, without entry, without innocence. What do I want with her? Inwardly I plead: Don't go away! . . . But in a minute the door will open and *I* will go away. . . . What is she doing here at *my* hour? Have I made a mistake? No, she. Or maybe she is Dr. Orrick's daughter, here to see him for a minute during the break. No . . . no, not his daughter. Too dressed up, too much on edge, too much like me. She's a patient. Oh God, I don't want her to go. What can I say?

"Excuse me, are you here to see Dr. Orrick?"

She looks up reluctantly . . . slight offense at the intrusion. "No."

Didn't get very far with that. What else can I say? What do I *want* with her? What, if I had her, would I do with her? My heart, with each caged and desperate beat, flutters out a wordless code of misery.

"Was afraid I'd made . . . a mistake," I say lamely. She does not look up. I'll give up my time, I think. I'll sit here and watch her. I won't leave her. From Dr. Orrick's office comes the sound of voices, footsteps. The young woman closes her magazine, now eagerly, perhaps anxiously, expectant. The time is at hand.

Nothing happens. The silence grows heavier. I cannot recall my devouring gaze. It makes her nervous. I feel a vast and desolate hunger, want to know her in most intimate detail, all that has happened to her, her entire life.

Why is she here? What does she suffer? Does she have a toothache? I visualize the tooth, her tongue touching it gingerly. Then my tongue enters the dark red cavern, caresses the tooth. Is she alone? Whom has she loved, why has it not worked out? If it had been I it would have worked out. I would never have left her. What does she fear? What does she desire?

The door opens. A man appears. Bushy hair. Pin-stripe suit, navy blue. The young woman is on her feet, smiling, locks arms with him. They leave together.

SEX is our tie to the world, the source of meaning. It drives us out of ourselves into engagement with the world. Because it is the nature of this drive to endow another— an *other*—with importance. And since this important other, becoming ever more enticing, spellbinding, this eventually supremely valuable other, lives and moves out there in the world, among the people and patterns and practices of the world, and because it is there she must be sought if ever she is to be found, the world itself, its forms and patterns and practices, has value and we attend to it.

PREOCCUPIED with Annette. Lovely Annette. Yet do not know her, have seen her but once, at the tennis courts, have spoken to her only a few words, would not recognize her on the street. Nevertheless, nevertheless . . . my desires clamor hungrily after her cloudy image like hounds after a fox.

What I pursue, endlessly, is not *out there* in *her*—in any her—but in me. It is a vision of love of which I comprise one half, and seek forever the other half. What I project onto her is a longing reciprocal to my own. It is my own longing experienced as coming back to me. What I desire so desperately, I already have. It is in me, my very own. Only aimed in the wrong direction, an arrow flying outward from my heart towards some other, while I yearn that it come flying from some other back to me. Where is that lover who will send her arrow into my heart—that I may die of love?

What started this was the phone call last night, a brief exchange to arrange a tennis game. Her "Hello" was neutral; I identify myself. "Oh yes!" She laughs, slight embarrassment; the timbre of voice, the quality of laugh, is warm with that kind of recognition that indicates she has been thinking of me. That's enough. Just that. I am instantly persuaded that a gleaming arrow such as the one I hold so restlessly, so ready and so eager to aim, is forming itself in her and aiming at my heart.

This is not love. Love is the caring that two people manage to negotiate between their yearnings to be one and the conflicts which would drive them apart. What I feel is pure yearning. There is no *other* out there. My Annette is a phantom. The real Annette is unknown to me, and when she comes to be known will disappoint me.

THE agitation of this yearning will drive me to madness. How much can one endure? I am a magnet in a world of wood, of ivory, of diamonds, cardboard, and snow. But no metal! No metal! Will I never feel that rushing together? that flying into one another's arms, that binding together, that blinding fusion, wholeness?

DESIRE increases with despair: measure the one, you measure also the other. Hunger for women grows as the capacity to satisfy it diminishes.

XI ✎

Impasse

I AM not of this world. Its purposes enlist no energies of mine, its remedies do not avail. But one does not judge all. The all must judge the one. In principle. In fact the world doesn't care, will not bother to judge, indifferently accepts my facade of adaptation.

HAVING for some time now been unable to act, there is nothing for it but to look back along the way I have come, to retrace and to examine the steps which led to this roadblock, to look for the wrong turn; or, should this prove, after all, to have been the right path, to find the means to dismantle the block and move ahead.

THINKING about living.
What does that mean? Reflecting on the experience of

living? Or standing apart, wondering whether to jump in? I mean the former, but it's well the ambiguity admits the latter; for thinking usurps the action it ponders. The moment passes. We are hurled forward. The road not taken is lost.

My books are too inward. I delve deeper and deeper into the soul, move further and further from the real world. I'm diving into the interior in pursuit of some retreating value, trying to catch hold before it disappears altogether. My work becomes more special, idiosyncratic, unpopular. My readers fall away. Few are willing to be led so far into the cave, not by the most mellifluous voice. With the next book I'll be alone, I feel it coming. Even my editor will desert me, while I go deeper, holding aloft my little candle, still talking, bearing witness to the dark shapes I am passing, unaware that my last follower has turned back, that my careful travelogue floats on empty air, finds no ears but my own.

I want to write about actual experience, the tangible, visible, smellable world, the world out there with its *things* and, above all, its people. Those things, people, events, happenings, interactions, developments—all that can be seen and touched and understood—that's the world. Why is it so dim? Why can't I invest it with value? make it vivid?

I'm pulling at the rug I stand on. My vision is the subsidence, the draining away, of value as of a precious fluid from the leaves, stems, stalks, and trunks of things and of human experience, leaving something thin, transparent, weightless. I search in vain for the opaque.

The material to be shaped is not words, but the world and what happens in it. This is for the writer what stone is for the sculptor, color for the painter. I am a sculptor whose marble has undergone a mysterious transformation during the years when he was learning to work it. Now when he really knows how, it crumbles in his hand. I am the painter who, having after some decades of work learned what can be done with pigments, finds all his colors drifting to gray. I can work only with material that retains in itself some inherent value, some interest, something to seek out, pursue, refine. I can't find this in the everyday world of things and of human experience. I find it, if at all, only in dark, disappearing shapes, something that has retreated far inward, far from the real world. It is now nothing more perhaps than a little dampness down at the roots. Maybe there is, down there, still a little bit of that value from which, if I am both diligent and lucky, I may yet distill a few drops, a little vial of what once was abundant in the world.

I CANNOT grasp the world by groping outward. I can reach it if at all only by a detour, a journey into the interior.

I GO through life seeking some extraordinary good, ignoring those goods commonly available in the give and take of human relations. Not the standard currency of human exchange but the pure gold of unconditional love.

Absolute selfless adoration, that's what I want. Only that would heal the wound at the center, make me whole.

I WALK about the house, can't sit still. It feels like home yet not like home. It's too still, too quiet. I look out on the smeared roofs of the houses below and want something to happen, want to go somewhere. I'm like my own father in his last days.

As a young man my father built a big house. Union Parish, Louisiana. Lived there with my mother for fifty years. In the same house. He was eighty-three when she died . . . went downhill fast. Became silent, restless, would wander about the house, looking for something, he didn't know what . . . would get dressed as if he were going somewhere. Black suit, white shirt, black string tie, cane, hat. Would sit on the front porch in the swing, waiting, looking for something. Talked to himself, nobody could understand what he was saying.

He would seek me out, tug on my arm. "I'm ready now, son, I want to go home." "You *are* home, Poppa," I would tell him; "this *is* home." I'd take him into his room, show him his clothes, his pipes, his bed. He would nod absently, would go back out on the front porch, sit in the swing, resume his waiting. And after a while he'd be back, tapping on my shoulder, a restless shuffle in his high laced black shoes, a feverish alienation in his eyes. "I want to go home now, son." "All right, Poppa. I'll take you home." He'd put on his hat and I'd take him by the arm, help him down the steps, out the front walk, through the gate, would hoist him up into the old Chevy. Then

I'd drive around town . . . would stop at Spence Allen's place. "Is that home, Poppa?" He would shake his head and we'd go on. I'd stop at Grover Hopkins' place. "Is this home, Poppa?" He'd look it over carefully and shake his head. I'd keep driving around, slowly, to all the places he knew. And he would keep looking. "When you see a place that looks like home, Poppa, just say the word and I'll let you out." And he would nod and brush his fingers against his lips, always quivering a bit, and would keep looking while I drove around the parish. Sometimes he would discover in some faint overgrown path into the woods a promise of the haven he sought, "Try down there, son." And I'd turn in until stopped by underbrush and fallen trees. And on and on. And of course he wouldn't find it, and finally I'd drive back home. "Is this it, Poppa?" "I guess so, son," he would say, beginning to climb down, disappointment in his voice. And I'd take him into the house and for a while he'd be content. But not for long. The next day he would get his cane and his hat and be tugging at my arm again. "I want to go home, son."

FIVE years old, too young for school. Skinny arms and legs sticking out from skimpy pants and short-sleeve shirt. When the older boys got back from school I went to Jimmy's house to play. Five boys had arranged themselves in a circle, were throwing a ball one to another in sequence. I put myself in the circle, but when my turn came the ball sailed over my head to the next in line. An oversight, perhaps; I waited the next round. When passed over again, I complained. They did not seem to hear. My complaint

grew louder, became pleading. Again and again the ball
flew over my head. I jumped but could not reach it,
wailed, went to my friend who usually was willing to play
with me, tugged on his sleeve, "Let me play, Jimmy!
Throw it to me too! Please, Jimmy!" Jimmy shrugged,
threw the ball over my head. I began to cry. "It's not
fair!" I was enraged, wanted to retaliate, to walk away.
But could not reject them so long as they would not see
me, would not hear. And because they were denying my
existence I could not give up trying to enter their circle.
I began to run after the ball, tried to intercept throws, but
when I managed to position myself before the next receiver,
the order would change, the ball going instead to someone else. I ran back and forth, in and out, never finding
a way to become a part. It was a magic circle, it joined
them, excluded me. I was a non-person.

Eventually I gave up, sat down at some distance,
exhausted, disheartened, watched the ball fly around, one
to another, in sequences of infinite desirability. It was too
painful to watch, I lowered my head, scratched in the
dirt. When my crying stopped, the boys tired of the game,
stood about idly, bored, wondered what to do next. "Here,
Henny," Jimmy said, as if to a dog, and tossed me the
now unwanted ball. The boys huddled, came to a decision, set off together. "Where are we going?" I asked,
following after. But again could not make myself heard.
I ran to keep up, but they ran faster, and came presently
to a thicket which, with their long pants, they could push
through, whereas I, with bare legs, was turned back
bleeding. The boys disappeared, their laughter grew fain-
ter, died away. I extricated myself from the brush, walked

back toward Jimmy's house. It was getting dark. There was a strong and cold wind. I was whimpering. Maybe crying.

Then there was my mother standing before me in her long brown coat. "A norther has come up," she said, taking my hand. "All of a sudden. That's why it's so dark and cold." I looked up. Black clouds were rushing across the sky. She wiped my nose. "We must go home." The pebbles hurt my bare feet; I hopped and lurched, holding her hand, trying to avoid the sharper stones. My teeth were chattering, the skin of my arms and legs became goose flesh. My mother stopped, opened her coat. "Come inside," she said. She folded me into the coat, buttoned it in front of me. We proceeded awkwardly, my shoulder against her thigh, my head alongside her hip, enveloped in darkness, in warmth, in the smell of her body. She was wearing an apron,and there was a smell also of food— onions and something fried. She must have been cooking supper when the norther hit. And stopped to come get me.

It was difficult to walk, we went slowly. I couldn't see anything ahead, but looking down could see the ground where I was putting my feet. I was getting warm in that germinal darkness. My teeth stopped chattering, my knees stopped shaking. I was aware of the powerful movement of her hip against my cheek, the sense of a large bone moving under strong muscles. Aware also that it was difficult for her to walk with me buttoned in. Occasionally she stumbled. And just then, for the first time, I became aware of goodness. Of goodness as a special quality, like evil, which a person may or may not possess. She doesn't *have* to do this, I thought. It's not necessary. I'm cold, but I could make it home all right.

What she gave me could not have been demanded, I would never have thought to ask. All afternoon I had been demanding something to which it seemed I had a right, and had been denied; yet here was a good to which I had no right, freely offered. No trade. Nothing asked in return.

THE meaning of life is in that coat; it is the home to which one belonged as a child. If you're lucky you never lose it, it simply evolves, smoothly and continuously, into that larger, more abstract home of religion, or perhaps, in a secular vein, into clan or community or ideology. Meaninglessness means homelessness. When home is lost and the nightmares begin, that's when one goes in quest of meaning.

And one has the impression then of reaching outward and forward, of delving into something *out there*, of grappling with the world, trying to penetrate a mystery; and it seems that one has only just come to recognize the existence of this most fundamental problem, a problem that has been there all along, but that only now, just possibly, one has arrived at the capacity to solve, or at least to try. But this is retrospective falsification. The problem has not been there all along; it came into being only with the loss of home, and the attempt to solve it is not an effort to create something new but to recreate something old.

It is a quest backward. One is trying to refashion, in a form acceptable to an intellectualizing adult, the home of one's childhood.

How to live? Who knows the question knows not how. Who knows not the question cannot tell.

I LISTEN to Mahler. The first theme is given by the violins, a sustained octave tremulo leading into a wispy melody, elusive, vanishing; the second theme, a dogged relentless march in C minor, comes from the horns. The two begin to interact, to illumine each other, to expand. The listener gains a sense of what the composer intends, the task he has set for himself; a structure emerges, can be analyzed, measured, talked about. But is not all. For gradually, as one listens also to other works by this composer, one begins to hear something else. A tone, unique and mysterious.

All writers repeat themselves. Is it not true that any writer, even the greatest—perhaps especially the greatest—has but one message? Is this not true of all artists? Can we not hear the same statement about the world and human life through all nine of Beethoven's symphonies or Mahler's? Who, knowing Mahler's other work, would fail after but a few measures of the Fifth Symphony to identify its author? Who, never before having heard "The Swan of Tuonela," would not instantly recognize the voice of Sibelius? Or, in the *Rosenkavalier* Waltzes, the bitter-sweet tenderness of Strauss?

This tone is not to be identified with instrument, with melody or rhythm, but arises from some interweave of

sonic elements, itself beyond formula or capture. We
achieve more than we intend. It is the sound drawn by
the bow of life across the composer's heart, is like a fin-
gerprint, a voice, a face. It can be imitated, but it cannot
authentically be generated by anyone else. It is a measure
of the risk the artist takes, of how deep into himself he
reaches, is the mark of one who reaches very deep indeed,
who works not just with the resources of which he is conscious, which he can call up and deploy at will, but who
goes all the way, spends it all, thereby imprinting the
work with a quality of self over which he has no control.
At that reach it is not what he knows or what he can do
that counts, but what he is. This is the meta-theme, the
unchosen, which infuses all chosen themes with such
vitality and meaning as they may acquire.

WHEN a writer comes to analysis, it's always because
he can't write. If he could, he'd handle whatever is wrong
by writing. That's what it's for. Death of children, loss of
wife—it's all grist for the mill. A mill that will accept
anything, any misery, depravity, crime, will grind it up,
mold it into literature. The author feeds it the despair of
his life, available usually in copious supply, and whatever the value to the world of the product, the process of
grinding it out is the writer's salvation. But when the mill
stops and the misery piles up, that's when they come to
analysis.

Writer and psychoanalyst are but two faces of the same
vocation, the attempt to work out one's own problems by
working on the problems of others. Real others for the

psychoanalyst; for the writer, imaginary others—or so he would have his family and friends believe. The psychoanalyst conducts his vicarious self-therapy in private; the writer invites the whole world to sit in on his sessions.

Should *I* go back into analysis? With an analyst who, perhaps, is himself blocked and who also has gone back into analysis? This thing could go full circle and, somewhere down the line, analyst number seven or eight might show up at *my* door to work on *his* block.

I DREAM that I have won a contest, something of great distinction, like the Nobel Prize. I am given the opportunity to address the world on television. A full hour, any subject, a year to prepare. I settle down to work, make sketches, rough drafts. Nothing seems right. I keep trying, keep discarding. Time slips by, weeks, months. It's getting very close. The time is at hand, I'm still not ready. My notes are a jumble, incomplete, I'm not sure what to say, how to begin. Limousine to the studio. Make-up man fussing around me. Spotlights, camera, countdown. The program director drops his arm as at the start of a race. The red light goes on. I see myself on a screen, I'm on the air, all over the world. Satellites in orbit are bending their electronic ears and eyes to carry my message. The second hand of the big clock begins its sweep of the first minute. I make a sound, a strangled, crushed syllable. Can't get it out. I'm choking. The program director says, "O.K., O.K., we'll take a break while you get it together." On the screen I see my image replaced by three girls plugging beer. Foam rises up in the mugs, they grin and mince and prance and sing their little ditty, while I struggle with my notes, try to get my thoughts together. Every now and then the program director checks back to see if I'm ready, the camera swings around, and I appear briefly on the screen, distraught, disorganized, notepaper slipping away, pencil falling to the floor; then the camera shifts, and it's those commercials that are getting sent around the world, inane, meritricious jingles to the millions who hunger for truth, for inspiration. And so the minutes slip by, on and on and on. The hour is almost over. Yet even in the few minutes remaining, one might still say something worth while. I struggle with my papers, sweat runs down my face, again the camera shifts to me, and still I'm mute, and the last few seconds are swept away.

XII ✒

Voices from the
Couch I

THE session dragged, the patient droned, the doctor dozed. The patient fell silent. The doctor roused himself. He had read somewhere—what was it? something about the CIA—that if you would understand a man you must find out what he desires. "What do you desire?" the doctor said.

"Girls," the patient said.

THE clocks tick. The lace curtains billow softly in and out. The gray fog muffles the sounds of traffic. Voices from the couch well up and flow over me. Voices of longing, bafflement, and desire.

THERE'S *a house in Berkeley where, on Saturday night, you pay ten dollars to get in, then you can fuck anybody you like. Full of girls. The ten bucks is for the wine and cheese and clean-up. The fucking is free. The girls do it for fun. Everybody just having a good time. . . . But I can't go. It's too late. They're all young. Twenties, thirties, maybe early forties. Might not even let me in. I'd be grandpa to them. Maybe they have such a place for senior citizens, reduced admission like for the movies, just show your Medicare card, walk right in and get laid. Not for me. I want to go where the young girls are. . . . It never changes. My skin sags, thins out, wrinkles, but the object of my desire is eternally the same, stands there in the first blush of youth. Years pass, decades, nothing happens to her skin. The turgor and the tenderness never change. The elastic fibers are all squeaky and new, the baby fat around the ass is smooth as silk. I want to be where she is. I don't want a geriatric bordello. . . . But I can't. Even if they would let me in. It's too late. I can get it up but can't keep it up. When I was young I couldn't keep it down. At a dance—oh I was far too shy to press it against a girl!— I'd pull back so she wouldn't feel it. I thought it was something to be ashamed of. Would go to great lengths to keep it from showing, would look for a post or a high-back chair to stand behind. Now it sleeps the sleep of the dead, or the almost dead. Won't perform at all without champagne and a string orchestra and a peep show. And even then it's very delicate. Have to hit a homer right away or the game is called.*

But maybe I'm still making excuses. That's what I want to know, what I've got to figure out. Lost youth is lost. Living already missed is missed for good. Looking back, I see only cowardice. The girls I could have had and passed up. Always there was a good reason, the best. Now every one of those reasons seems false, and every one of those missed girls a waste of life. In the name of fidelity, of decency, but really weak knees. I want to know whether I'm still doing the same thing.

My erotic history is one long list of misses. Girls wanted but not had. Not the ones that got away. That doesn't bother me. That I can accept—if I tried and failed. What galls is the not having tried. The lowered head, the darkly sweeping lashes, the swinging curls, the shy smile, the quick backward glance—that's the memory that drives me crazy! Time after time. Offers! Offers! They wanted it, and I knew it, and I wanted it, and stood there rooted to the spot, rooted in a crazy asceticism, let them slide away, wasted, wasted. I regret every one, want them back. I want to go back to each moment of opportunity, change my reaction, accept. Accept! They're old women now. It's not possible. Or maybe it is but I don't want them. I want them now as they were then. As their daughters are now. As—God help us!—their granddaughters are now.

At home, in the dark, under the covers, the meat and potatoes of conjugal grappling, ever more boring, passion and ecstacy evaporating like carelessly stoppered perfume, leaving only ejaculation, which never evaporates, at least not for me, still necessary, but more and more resented, the wifely cunt gradually drying up, becoming less and less available. And every day in the streets and offices, in elevators, aeroplanes, supermarkets, flower shops, banks, everywhere, those girls with darkly swinging hair, the passion that evaporated from marriage condensing on them in a dew of wild yearning that won't go away, that does not diminish with age. . . . Always there was a reason not to do it—moral or medical or God knows what, something to do with dignity or seriousness or commitment or the higher things of life. I don't believe a word of it. All rationalization. It was not the higher things of life, but fear. Fear of my bloody superego with its scourge, its vindictive stare, its hostility toward impulse.

IF we don't want it we can have it, like the air we breathe, effortlessly, in unlimited amount; but if we desire it deeply, if it stalks our days and nights, like that dark-haired woman who beckons in my dreams, we shall find it never. The dice are loaded, the same numbers keep turning up, the way it works out for us suits an alien purpose.

I feel the flick of an ancient whip, the whip that drove my forebears through all those eons, drove them howling and heartsick after all those unattainable women, or, when attainable, through one after another of them until, broken and spent, they found one finally who *was* unattainable upon whom then could be concentrated what was left of their repeatedly broken hearts. I should shout out: "Brothers! Brothers! Take heed! We are rushing on to despair and madness in pursuit of something chosen for us to want but not in our interest to want. Like cattle we go forward, blinded in uproar and dust, thinking we are seeking what *we want*. But brothers! it is not *we* who want all those women—one or two would be enough— but a force that ignores our interest, our welfare, that would sacrifice every one of us, to a man, in a moment, without a pause, without a glance, to achieve its iron purpose. Take heed! It's a biological trick. We have been selected for desiring. Nothing could have convinced us by argument that it would be worth while to chase endlessly and insatiably after women, but something has transformed us from within, a plasmid has invaded our DNA, has twisted our nature so that now this is exactly what we *want* to do. But we did not choose a nature that would have such wants, that would send us careening after women, fatuously, self-destructively, through all the days of our lives. Never, never would we, looking at the consequences, choose such a lemming nature. It was pressed upon us while we slept. We must rise up, reject it."

The cry is futile. No one heeds. Not even *I* can heed. The transformation is in the seed. We can sometimes throw off modes of behavior acquired on the basis of what we are but cannot throw off what we biologically are. There's no place to stand. However we turn or dodge or run it's right there with us, in us, twisting our heads to follow the clicking of those high heels, those slender ankles, the swaying skirt, that fluid roll of hips, the dark hair, the mysterious eyes that beckon and betray.

VIOLATION *is part of my desire, the dark underside. Might be better not to know. But I do know. The garden must be secret, guarded, mysterious. Access must be hidden or difficult or denied. I seek to enter where, though I be desired, I'm not altogether welcome. Resistance must be overcome. Some advantage, not entirely fair or honorable, must be taken.*

The veiled face, that's the archetype. It signals both resistance and invitation, the one as important as the other. Of course that veil has been displaced upward. It's really the genital that is veiled, and the veil is to be rent. Not the open, smiling face. Not the pretty cheerleader at a football game with bare legs, prancing about, grinning; but the elegant lady in velvet and fur glimpsed for but a moment as she gets out of a cab. Or, better, from a carriage. Carriage? Why is that better? Because in the days of carriages gardens were better guarded, their despoilation more difficult, hence a keener pleasure. The driver stops the horses before a handsome three-story house with shuttered windows, an air of mystery; the door of the carriage opens, a little boy gets out, a muffled cry from within, the boy turns back, a woman leans out, lifts her veil—the veil! that's central—she clasps the boy to her breast, kisses him wildly, her face covered with tears. Why tears? What does that add? I've come upon her in a moment of weakness; and that weakness nourishes my wish to violate, adds a pulse of hope.

Another image. A woman I've known and liked for a long time, attractive, friendly, but never desired by me. Has been quite ill but has turned a corner, is beginning her recovery. I go to visit her in the hospital. As I enter the room she is standing by the bed in her nightgown, hair undone and unbrushed, hanging to her waist. It's her first attempt to walk, she's very wobbly. She smiles at me with a trace of helplessness and bewilderment. I embrace her, and, feeling her body against mine within that filmy gown, am suddenly stunned by a jolt of desire. Those shaky legs, that tangled hair—they signal a lapse of defense, call up my wish to ravish.

I'm not talking about rape. It's no good unless the woman wants it too, at least a little. I'm talking about something subtle and insidious. Even when she presses against me—any woman I mean, not my friend in the hospital—pelvis tilting forward and upward, thighs spreading, wanting it. Even then there is violation. Must be. For that moment can have come about only by the overcoming in her of something that wants to keep her closed. It is overcome by an opposing force in her which is my ally and which I have evoked. Something faintly evil. It will lead her ultimately to waste herself rather than to conserve herself. What she ought to do—what her father would want for her—would be to send me packing. The garden should remain inviolate. But I have cast a spell, have beguiled her away from that native caution, that self-protectiveness, have stirred into life another force which will persuade her to let me in. By her submission I conscript her to the sacrifice of self to my desire—eventually to pregnancy, to children, to the ongoing life process which will use her up and fling her aside.

I can't believe it's this way for women. They don't want to violate a man. Were one of them to approach me with the motivation I bring to them I'd run for my life. Or for my soul! What they want must be something quite different. They want to be talked to. I know what they want. They want to be understood, to be known in their specialness, to be truly recognized.

Here is an image. A girl with straight dark hair, always brushed to a fare-you-well, something secret and private in her manner, always friendly but reserved, a faint quality of distrust. We have a casual acquaintance. We pass often in the hall, we nod. She smiles. Graphic arts, that's what she does for a living. And what's that? Who knows? Who cares? Well . . . if I want to get into her pants I had better care. I do want to. "Some day, when you have time," I say to her, "I'd love to see your studio. I really don't know what it is you do. I'd like to see your work." She's willing, though a bit surprised, is curious about my interest, a little suspicious. We make a date. At the studio she is shy, points out a few things, "This is what I'm working on now. It's not finished, though. You really can't tell." She doesn't say much. But I say a lot. I ask questions. Real questions. I enter into her experience, I seek out the problems inherent in each of her projects, what she is struggling with, I try to get the feel of them, to figure out how her designs, her inventions, have solved these problems . . . or have failed to solve them, or have solved them in part. I enter another life, understand it. And I convey to her my recognition. And all this, if I am sincere, will be an interesting experience for me. I'll learn something new. But this was not my object, is not for me essential. I could live without it. But for her what's happening there between us is essential, it meets her deepest need, is life-giving, rescues her from anonymity, bestows significance, brings her individuality alive. She sees herself in a clearer light. The giver of that experience becomes terribly important to her.

Now, then—here perhaps I contract time, we may need

one or two more meetings—we have finished our tour of
the studio. I take her hand, move closer. I want now a
tour of the secret garden. And now she is in trouble. The
garden, as she knows very well, is off limits, no one is to
enter, she holds it in trust, is custodian but is not to admit
visitors. Especially not casual visitors. But she is grateful
to me, is also afraid of losing me. If she says no, perhaps
I will go away, will take back the great gift of recognition.
She is in conflict. And as she hesitates I press her close,
my lips touch hers, she finds my tongue making a sugges-
tion, my hand stealing down along the curve of breast,
brushing the nipple, down her flank to the shaded slope
above the garden. Her thighs are still pressed together, yet
she is beginning now to feel something more than gratitude, more than the fear of losing me. There is a welling
up in her of a desire to open, to take me in, to fuse with
me, to receive deeply what I want to plant; and this is all
mixed up in her with that hunger for recognition which
still presses on her, insatiable; and maybe—she thinks,
she hopes—that recognition and understanding can be
carried by the sexual union to an even deeper fulfillment.
This confusion in her, this mixture of desire and gratitude
and hope of self-realization, all this is drawing her away
from her guarded self, from her position of trust. The inner
muscles of her thighs, so rigid but minutes ago, now soften,
the thighs fall apart, I am in the garden:

    There has been no force, she is a free agent, she lets me
in, but I know myself a despoiler. And—to squeeze out
from this obscure truth the last bitter drop—the more
immaculate the garden where my muddy boots now tread,
the greater the victory, the deeper my gratification.

This violation gets filtered out in marriage. It becomes shameful, is excluded. It's a lie that the full range of physical love can be realized in marriage. Conjugal love has comforts and advantages, and convenience, but this transcendent passion, dependent on a trace of predation, it has not. When a man has free access, the garden no longer secret, there is no remaining mystery. When it stands open, is repeatedly known, when he enters at will, traverses the same old paths, comes time and again upon the same old vistas, then he is in the realm of daily bread, of affection and security, of a "good relationship." And all that may be very good indeed, may be the best we can hope for, and it may be that a wise man would settle for such. All that may be true. But it's not true that it's the same as that first knowing, that primal surrender and that primal violation. Not only does this not occur in marriage, it's not possible in principle. It's a lie. It's the publicity line for the guardians of our sacred institutions who would have us believe that a faithful marriage does not entail the giving up of something magical and mysterious in the life of the flesh.

BECAUSE sexuality entails for man, but not for woman, a necessary violation, it is marked for man with unavoidable guilt. Without violation nothing would happen. Life would stop. Someone must move close, invade the intimate space of another.

Love is born of sin. Love without sin is not enough; sin without redemption is unbearable. She must come to love me, including—and this is central—that part of me which *wants* to violate her. She must love me entire. This is the transforming acceptance. I am reborn, become, that rare thing, both whole and innocent. What Christ on the cross did for mankind she, in bed, in this carnal age, must do for me.

But nothing is forever. Redemption wanes. Innocence is lost, wholeness is lost, guilt surges up, the self is split. The same act with the same partner loses its ritual power. Girl becomes wife, knows what I would do to her, accepts it, perhaps gladly, perhaps even with pleasure. There is no barrier to break through, no veil to tear, no violation, no sin. Therefore no forgiveness, no redemption. I begin to look about with desire, am burning for something forbidden. So freighted, love cannot be a simple beneficence that comes naturally like spring rain, becomes a driven pursuit upon which life itself depends.

Sin is the primal assumption of Christianity, and it is Christianity that elevates love into the means of salvation. For a thousand years it was the love of Christ that redeemed our sin collectively; then, as Christianity began to wane, it became the exalted love of one woman that redeemed one's individual sin. When God hides his face social redemption is lost, sin encrusts our lives in a deathly patina, romantic love gains in importance. Deserting the common life, it attempts realization in the private realm of a hunger for meaning that can be satisfied, if at all, only in the common realm.

SITTING *in an orange deck chair on brightly green grass, newly mown, near a swimming pool. Oleander blossoms around me, pine branches above me. A woman sitting at the pool pulls off a rubber cap, shakes out her long black hair. Guilt is subsiding. Fantasies of transgression surge up again.*

COULD it be that the wish to violate a woman issues from that part of self that was split off because it once entailed the loss of one's mother's love? If so, the wish would be aiming to recover and affirm this lost part of self. And if the woman, suffering the violation, still loves the violator, then that lost part of self need not again be repressed, but may be reclaimed, restored.

Does not something like this happen in analysis? The analyst makes it possible for the patient to recover and express the previously split-off anger; and though himself the innocent object of that anger, (innocent? who is innocent?) he remains attached, thereby enabling the patient to integrate that anger with the rest of his emotional life and so become whole?

Such a view of therapy echoes the Christian scheme of salvation. Christ offered himself as a sacrifice to man's demonic rage. "Father, forgive them; for they know not what they do." His unconditional love redeems those who believe, they recover their true selves, are born again.

A FEARLESS woman is without attraction. Admirable perhaps, worthy, resourceful, a loyal friend, all those good things; but for that magic that pulls us on, sucks our hearts out, she must be vulnerable.

I will never forget the Spanish girl. Blue uniform, like an airline hostess. Small blue pillbox cap on her head, straight brown hair to the level of her chin, one strand falling across her right eye as she lowers her head. Enormous dark liquid eyes. Great shyness. Afraid to look, to make eye contact, yet willing if it is required, then quickly the frightened smile, the averted gaze.

"But *it's so* vulgar!" *she says to me.*

"So?" I say. "Life is vulgar. Pursuit of the vulgar is loyalty to life. One of these days I'll learn to enjoy farting. . . . On second thought, I enjoy it already. One of these days I'll just be more open about it."

She puts on her martyr face. "This is gutter talk. You're not like that. You have always been one to search for the spiritual."

"I was brainwashed. The gutter is all there is."

When I was a boy we lived on a farm. The outhouse was rickety, damp, rank with urine, shit, and lime. A basket of crinkled squares of tissue paper, the paper oranges used to be wrapped in. I remember once, having shat, standing up and looking down the hole, seeing a faint glimmer of liquid surface. Then, as the sun aligned itself with a crack in the footing, a shaft of light revealed that surface to be, not still as I had supposed, but alive, writhing with maggots. In the stillness I could hear the faint licking sounds of their movements in the muck. I stared with the fascination of one who sees the future. We rise up out of the earth and assume the shape of God. Briefly, briefly. Then down in the earth again. The handful of me I had just dropped in that pit was already being transformed into maggots, and presently they would get the rest of me. I would become them. Their writhing would be my writhing.

In the meantime, then, in that crack of light, as Nabokov puts it, between two eternities of darkness, maybe the best we can do is our own special writhing together which alone has the power to blot out for a moment the darkness and the worms.

XIII ⟋⌒◦

Voices from the Couch II

Once I was three weeks in a Boy Scout camp. In the woods by a river. About two hundred boys, twelve to fifteen, and a dozen counsellors, seventeen to twenty. We spent the days canoeing, rubbing sticks, building fires, making arrow heads, earning merit badges, that sort of thing. We had meals in the mess hall at long wooden tables. At one end of the hall was a raised platform where the Commandant and the senior counsellors ate. The Commandant was a tall man, stern and unsmiling, a retired army captain, walked about with a riding crop, always checking up on the counsellors who were supposed to be always checking up on us. We slept four to a tent and there was to be no jerking off. The Commandant was determined to "stamp that out," gave talks on the dangers of "self-abuse." The camp was run along military lines, everything by bugle call. We got up to reveille, went to bed to taps. Most of us came from poor families. It cost *ten dollars a week to be there, and a session was three weeks. Sunday was visiting day, families had the noon meal with us, spent the afternoon being shown around, left about five o'clock.*

One Sunday evening we gathered for supper, seated ourselves at the long tables. The food was before us but we were not permitted to touch it until the Commandant said grace. He waited so long, glowering over our heads, we knew something was up. The counsellors shot warning glances at us. When the hall was completely still the Commandant rose, but instead of pronouncing grace he began a little talk. It started off mildly enough, but from the beginning there was an ominous note.

"Last Sunday," he said, "I had the pleasure of meeting a lovely lady and her lovely daughter, the mother and sister of one of our scouts. It was their first visit to our camp. I had the pleasure of having lunch with this lovely lady and her lovely daughter. We had a long, uplifting talk, and later I showed them about the camp. They met many of you and talked to you, were most interested in all the things we are doing here. This lovely lady was particularly impressed by our goals and aspirations, by the high standards we seek to maintain, and by the ideal of honor which is the very heart of scouting. I told her all these things with great pride, pride in this camp, and pride in all of you. . . . Now I was very pleased, as you can imagine, to see this lovely lady again today. Also a little surprised, for she lives quite some distance and I had not expected her back so soon. She was alone this time, and one look at her told me this was no ordinary visit. In privacy and in great distress she told me what had happened.

On Wednesday the postman had delivered to her home a letter addressed to her lovely daughter. Fortunately, the daughter did not see it; the mother was able, by the grace of God, to intercept it." He paused, scanned his audience with heavy portentousness. "She gave me the letter to read." Slowly he raised aloft the letter. "It was written by one of the scouts in this camp." His face grew dark with passion, his voice throbbed. "It is the most odious letter I have ever read. It is a lascivious letter. It is a letter of vulgar language. It makes a vile proposal to that lovely girl. It is a disgrace to me personally and it is a disgrace to this camp." Slowly he crumpled the pages in his fist. "Is Philip Orlikoff present?"

In the shocked silence that followed, the boy was gradually identified by the many who—curiosity, as at a hanging, gaining over horror—looked at him. "Let him stand and come forward," the Commandant thundered. The boy was at the back of the hall, near the door. He stood, hesitated, then uncertainly walked down the center aisle. With a gesture the Commandant directed him to mount the platform. They stood face to face. The boy could not bear the Commandant's gaze, his head fell. He was short and slight, his legs trembled. "Philip Orlikoff," the Commandant intoned, "you have brought disgrace upon this camp and upon all of your fellow scouts. You have betrayed the solemn vows of scouting. You have taken the scout's honor and trampled it in mud and filth. You are a traitor. You are no longer a scout." He snatched the emblematic blue kerchief from the boy's neck, ripped the merit badges from his shirt, threw them to the floor. "I am directing your local scoutmaster, and also the national

office, to strike your name from our rolls. I order you now
to go directly to your tent, pack your belongings, and be
gone from this camp within twenty minutes, never to
return. You are dismissed." The stricken boy descended
the platform, came down the center aisle, his face white
and taut. Everyone watched him, he looked at no one.
The screen door closed behind him. He disappeared into
the summer night. We never saw him again. The Commandant then raised both arms forward to shoulder level,
closed his eyes. "Now may the grace of God be with us
once again. Bless this food that now we take for the nour-
ishment of our bodies. May we use our bodies only in
pursuit of Thy purposes. Deliver us from temptations of
the flesh. Amen."

You want a portrait of my superego? The Commandant is an exact copy. Vindictive, relentless. Implacable
hatred of impulse. Placation, indeed, because of its covert
acknowledgement of guilt, serving only to increase its sad-
ism. And would you want a snapshot of my id? It's that
letter with its leering proposition, its dirty words, that letter in the Commandant's hand, like a mouse in the talons
of a hawk. And my ego? You want that? Then you'll have
the whole picture, what you guys call the "tripartite psychic
structure." My ego is Philip Orlikoff as he walks back down
that aisle, bloodless, trembling, going out in disgrace into
an endless night of alienation. So there I am, the whole
of me, set forth in tableau, frozen in that mess-hall drama
of that long-gone summer evening. Scouting does in truth
build character!

So my dirty letters were never written, they remained
but fantasies. I was cowed by the Commandant. I never

propositioned anybody. Sex had to be redeemed by love, hallowed by marriage, before the Old Man would O.K. it. But now I know that every time I passed up a sexual opportunity in the name of higher values I was just cringing before the Commandant.

Now things have changed. The culture has changed. The Commandants are all gone. They have been laughed off the stage, replaced by dancing girls. License is proclaimed in newspapers, television, neon lights; you can take courses in touching and get college credit. Hot tubs are bubbling and the naked girls are laughing and dancing. And I have changed. It took quite a while but finally I rebelled, toppled the Commandant, usurped his power. So I and the culture have journeyed together, are both now free, the fun can begin. . . . Only for me, it can't. I'm too old. Sexual freedom arrives in a dead heat with physical incapacity. Like Moses, I've come a long way, can look into a promised land of stiff cocks and swollen cunts, but cannot enter!

Or can I? What is this? What is it now? More of the same? Maybe the Commandant isn't dead. Could it be simply that I now use age as before I used higher value? Still rationalizing cowardice? Or is it really too late?

LIKE the gray light that seeps through the lace curtains, rises as in a pool, and fills the room with muffled stillness, so longing, pain, and desire spill forth, accumulate, rise, wash over me, mount, fill the room, while I sit here alone in the still depths, feeling my way, in the dark, like a blinded ship at the bottom of a sea of fog.

WE *were sitting in the kitchen, had just finished breakfast. He began to shift about, cleared his throat. "We've been studying gynecology," he says to me, and coughs and fidgets. "Monday we start in the clinic. Examining patients. I thought maybe . . . if you don't mind . . . I'd like to examine you. For practice. To see how well I do . . . if I can recognize the landmarks."*

"I don't mind." Us married more than a year and him blushing! In the bedroom I took off my shoes, took off my panties, pulled up my skirt, lay down. He loomed over me, tube of lubricating jelly in one hand. "An examining table is so much higher," he says uncertainly. "Get down on your knees," I tell him. "Yes. That will help. . . . Maybe you'd better take off your skirt. I'm going to start with an abdominal examination. . . . Now . . . raise your knees a bit. Like that. . . . Now, relax. Breathe through your mouth." He poked about, very gingerly. "Any tenderness? . . . Tell me if anything hurts."

"You can push harder than that."

"Belly soft. Uterus and ovaries not palpable. No masses. No tenderness. Everything normal." He's dictating to a nurse. "Now, if you would raise your legs, please. . . . Hm, I guess we're going to have to get you a little higher." I put my feet on the bed, lift my hips, and he puts a folded pillow under my behind. "Now raise your legs again. Yes, that's better." He adjusts the lamp—to the field of his interest, you might say. "Now separate your legs. . . . As widely as possible. . . . That's good. . . . Now, let your head rest on the bed. Relax. . . . Perineum normal. No external hemorrhoids." He turns aside and from the corner of my eye I see him roll a white rubber sleeve over his

*middle finger. Then he is playing with my anus, running
the tip of his finger round and round to spread the lubricant. With astonishing ease, without force or friction, he
is up my ass, pushing into the lower part of my rectum.
"Just relax," he says calmly. Practicing his professional
manner, he was. "Open your mouth. Breathe deeply. Anal
ring normal. Internal sphincter normal. No internal
hemorrhoids. No adenexal masses." The nurse still taking
it all down we hope. Now the finger is out, the finger cot
is being discarded, a piece of tissue is produced—now that
was thoughtful of him—and he is wiping my ass, "Front
to back," he says.*

*"Now the external genitalia." He puts his left hand on
my knees, tilts my bottom a bit higher, opens me up. I
push my head back into the pillow, close my eyes, begin
to feel a pleasant buzz of excitement. "Mons normal, labia
majora normal, no inflammation, no exudate." Sounds
like a pilot with his checklist. First the outer lips, then the
inner, are gently pulled apart. I feel cool air on parts usually closed away. "Labia minora normal. Urethra normal. Clitoris normal." I feel a shot of intense pleasure as
he touches it.*

*He turns aside, is putting talcum powder on his right
hand, pulling on a rubber glove. His pants are bulging
with an enormous erection. He must have grown! I feel
lethargic, am both aroused and amused. He is playing
doctor! But of course. That's probably why he wants to be
a doctor. He'll have a state license to explore a woman's
body. His mother's body. Afraid to otherwise. "Now relax,"
he says again, and the rubber fingers are playing with my
vagina, spreading the lubricant. "Now . . ." His voice is*

hoarse. The fingers move slowly into my vagina. I feel the
stretch of my ring, know I can exclude him, squeeze him
out, if I wish. But do not wish, want him to enter, to
stretch me, to push deeper. "*Vault normal. Cervix hard*
and round and smooth. Now I have my finger on the cer-
vical os. Do you feel that?"

I do indeed. A *wonderful little fiddling around some-*
where deep inside. "*Yes . . . yes . . . yes . . . go on.*"

"*Anterior fornix normal. Posterior fornix normal. Slight*
retroversion." *His voice is cracking, he can hardly speak.*

A *wave is mounting in me, lifting me up, would throw*
me away. I open my eyes. He is leaning forward, his head
between my legs, close to my belly, his face darkly suf-
fused, veins standing out on his forehead. Then suddenly
I am flooding, my bottom contracting, while with both
hands I grab his wrist and thump his two fingers deeper
into me in time with the contractions. Oh it was heaven!
I moaned and rolled about, it went on a long time, and
finally I was finished.

A *large wetness was spreading on his pants. I laughed.*
"*You examine very well,*" *I say to him. He really did!* "*I*
hope you will learn to do it more objectively."

SEX shows, it occurs to me, are watched by silent staring men; there are no such houses filled with women
watching men being degraded, reduced to objects. Why
is that? . . . Castration anxiety my colleagues would say,
but that's too specific. It's more subtle . . . and more
pervasive. And maybe more simple. People are dangerous. That's enough. There is murder in our hearts.

Therefore intimacy is dangerous. We have good reason to be afraid. So better not get too close. Four or five feet would be about right. Room to dodge or run or strike back. That's what security would call for. But at that distance, no sex. The sexual drive pushes us closer. One of us has to move in, take the risk. One has to penetrate, the other receive, and in that embrace we cannot be defended.

But this danger does not fall evenly on the two. Since it is the man who pursues, who moves in close, it is he who must deal with this anxiety first. Because until he does, nothing will happen. The two of them will stay at a distance, eyeing each other. The woman can wait. She's in no hurry. If the man comes too close too fast, she can send him packing; only if he manages to diminish her anxiety will she allow him closer . . . and then closer, eventually to enter her.

Men gather in pornographic shows, not to stimulate desire, as they may think, but to diminish fear. It is the nature of the show to reduce the woman, discard her individuality, her soul, make her into an object, thereby enabling the man to handle her with greater safety, to use her as a toy, a doll. And since fear diminishes desire, the felt effect of reducing fear is increasing desire. That's why it's such a turn-on for a man to be standing upright with a woman kneeling before him. The embrace is broken, the woman forced down out of mutuality, becoming the one who serves. On her knees, her head bare to his fists, her vulnerability is total. And if perchance his fear is so great that even this is not enough, the pornographic houses will show him a woman chained and gagged.

As women move increasingly toward equality, the felt danger to men increases, leading to an increase in pornography and, since there are some men whose fears cannot even so be stilled, to an increase also in violence against women.

IN *the newspaper I come upon a new advertisement among the pornographic listings.* Marguerite in the Afternoon. *"It's refreshing in the morning, it's the bread of life at night, but have you tried it in the afternoon? With Marguerite?" The picture shows the upper part of a naked girl sitting in bed. Alone. Ornate bed, fancy room. Perhaps a bordello. Short blonde hair, face soft and pliant. No evidence of character. Quite young. Maybe seventeen. Features unfinished. Full lips, mouth slightly open, eyes averted, a dreamy look on her face. Perhaps masturbating. She is, I imagine, in her first awakening to passion. I feel the lust rise in my veins, in my mouth, can almost taste the free-running juices of this girl.*

I shift the paper, the light falls at a different slant, and I find myself looking at my daughter as she was at about fifteen. What had been a rumpled sheet beside the prostitute appears now as Jenny's teddy bear. It jars me. Something flips. I am rushing to her rescue.

I tilt the newspaper, find I can alter the image at will. From one angle the girl is a stranger, object of my lechery; from another, my daughter, claiming my protection. The shadow can be the rumpled sheet of abandon or the teddy bear of innocence, as I will. Shifting the picture back and forth, I realize that what is jarring me is not the changing image before me, but the changing orientation within. Each shift of image occasions violently opposed intentions. I am not one person perceiving something out there in one way or another, but am one person or another person depending on what seems to be out there. I position the paper to reflect my daughter, observe the inner configuration.

The girl is not an object of desire, is not an object at all. She is a person with a history, with memories, who had chicken pox while vacationing in Mexico, who came sleepwalking into my bedroom after her first day at school, who had a terrible time with algebra, who would slip her hand into mine and ask me to help her, who still, to this day, gnaws at her fingers, a person dear to me, with anxieties, longings, needs. She is still in high school, full of inexperience, doesn't belong in a bordello. I am appalled. It is wildly inappropriate that she be there. She has made a terrible mistake, has fallen into evil hands, is in trouble. How could those men, the ones who rumpled the sheets, how could they have done to her such things as I am forced by this setting to imagine? Had they no common decency? Could they not see she was a child? Did they not know this would destroy her? Did they not care? Anger is rising in me. I am moving up to the bed, am standing beside it, taking Jenny's hand. Now I turn, am facing the men who might still be wanting her, am denying her to them, making them ashamed of what they intended with her. Now I am telling her to get dressed, I am taking her out of here. No one will stop me. She will go back home with me, to her own room, will go back to school. When she finishes high school she will go on to college, will prepare herself for a vocation, for a way of life that will sustain self respect.

Now I position the paper to reflect the prostitute. She is quite young, but is awakened, not a virgin, has been through quite a few romps, is becoming wanton, yet still is in the first flowering, a bit bewildered by so much passion. That slight confusion and helplessness, that pliant vulnerability, excite me. No will of her own, I can do as I like. Her resistance, to anything, will be slight. I will override her objections, will ride her down. She will know she should stop me, yet will not. Something about me will make her want to give in, to do as I wish. I feel the mounting excitement of a hunter closing in on his prey; I don't want to hurt her, but to have her, to ravish her. I will be gentle. I sit on the bed, begin to stroke her face, her cheeks rounded like a child's, her short curly hair. She is a bit frightened but likes my touch. I move on to her breasts, her belly, gradually escalate my violation of her unspoken limits, move always toward the center, breaching the concentric defenses one after another, coming in from the perimeter, moving always toward the center. I play with her nipples, make them stand up, suck them, explore the crevices of her belly button. Her will is paralyzed, she cannot resist. I continue my excursions into ever more forbidden recesses, proceeding inexorably, as a foregone certainty known to us both, to that eventual pulling apart of her legs and plunging into her cunt. She is an object, not a subject. I see not her need, but her capacity to serve my need. And what is my need? To do to her something like what a farmer does to the land. Take it over, seize possession, plow into it, seed it, make it grow. The farmer does not trouble himself with whether it is in the interest of the

land to receive such treatment; nor do I with this pliant
young woman.

What about this, Doc? . . . You have any answers?
Am I doomed to be one or the other, protector or predator?
Is there no other way with her? Where is love? Indeed what
is love? And where in this scenario might it have appeared?
. . . I shift the paper, the fall of light alternating the images.
Is love the fusion of these two orientations? a fusion which
in my life has fallen apart? Or is it a third position
unknown to me, beyond my reach?

WHEN he views his daughter he enters a relationship,
deals with a person. When he views the prostitute he
abandons human relations, dismembers her, deals with
parts: breasts, buttocks, belly, genitals. She shatters like a
pane of glass into erotic shards, into mounds and curves
and apertures. What is he clawing after so desperately
over these surfaces? . . . For love? . . . With a shard?

We strain toward an unattainable closeness. No way
further to invade her, any her, no deeper plunge. We've
had our way with her, have done everything, yet desire
still clamors, is thrown back, baffled, by the gentle yielding flesh. One must give up. To go further is madness.

Madmen kill. It *must* be there, they think, somewhere
within that supple body . . . the secret, the mystery. Why
can it not be found or reached or touched? They won't
stop. But murder has no longer reach than love, and
madmen too are defeated, stand empty-handed, bereft,
before the dismembered body, the still-warm heart.

We drape fantasies over women, making them into

something they are not. They look up at us from magazines, the garment gapes, the flesh gleams; we see them from the rear, they glance back invitingly, shyly, alluringly, wearing rags and tags of black lace, bending over, pulling on a stocking. They are pure receptivity. They are *our* fantasies, yet look real, as if they were out there somewhere, to be found, and we believe that with such a one that merging, that oneness, might be possible. Maybe *she*—that one in the purple garter-belt—would welcome the pursuit, the capture, the being held close, being taken possession of, and all the rest of what we would want to do with her. And maybe *she* would, but she's not real. And if, in a fit of mad enterprise, we should contact the agent of that model, and eventually after much embarrassment should manage to meet her . . . she's wearing jeans, is reticent, opinionated, stubborn, a bit suspicious, doesn't even own a garter belt.

And even if, as the wildest improbability, we should find a woman who had become the fantasy . . . even then the sought-for closeness would not be possible. For the woman who really matched the fantasy would be empty. Nothing there.

YOU *know what Camus said about this? "It is difficult to return to the places of one's early happiness. The young girls in the flower of their youth still laugh and chatter on the seashore, but he who watches them gradually loses his right to love them, just as those he has loved lose the power to be loved." That's elegant and elegaic, and true, but it is not my condition. My trouble is the loss, not of the right* to love them, but of the ability to fuck them. No, that's not right either. It's the loss of the desire to love them, being left only with an itch to fuck them.

I'm ashamed, also angry and confused. What is this anyway? Do you guys have an explanation? Is this an infantile conflict—to be analyzed? Or the way things are— to be accepted? Why this degradation of the sexual drive? I've had this longing all my life, but it used to be something quite different. It was always sexual, I think, and perhaps the union of bodies was always the culmination. But it was not carnal. In essence it was spiritual. Ethereal. The raw energy of sexual drive, like fuel for a rocket, was used for loftier purpose and was able thereby to lift the longing into a higher realm. I was concerned with symbols—the dropped handkerchief, the veiled face, the red rose, the scented stationery, the way the letter was signed, even the way the stamp was affixed. Where has all that gone? I used to idealize a beautiful face. Greta Garbo, the expressive mouth with its minute quiver of vulnerability, the lashed and limpid eyes, their unplumbed and unfathomable depths. Marlene Dietrich, that domed and nunlike forehead. Margaret Sullavan, those candid eyes sweeping over me so close, like a touch, soul to soul, that husky voice, that exalted courage in one so frail. It would choke me up. Those were the things that swarmed in my mind. The yearning was for love, for melting into one another. I would never have permitted a word like fuck— or screw—to associate itself with my desire, and I would have turned in fury upon anyone who suggested that that was all it amounted to. I wanted love, I wanted the two of us to become so precious one to another that a crisis *calling for the sacrifice of life would come almost as a relief. A tragedy too, of course, since it meant a parting, but a relief in that it would enable me to prove in action what otherwise could only be professed: that I loved her more than life itself. Where has all that gone? That's what Camus talks about. Maybe he didn't live long enough to come upon the degradation of this yearning with age.*

But Evan Connell did. This is how he puts it, the kind of girl he's looking for. "Abandoned. Lascivious. Dissolute. The more dissolute the better. Everything that I am not but would like so much to be. A young lady experienced in each conceivable depravity, totally intemperate, unbuttoned, debauched, gluttonous, uncorked, crapulous, self-indulgent, drunken and preferably insatiable. Never mind if it is an adolescent dream, never mind. There may be no such woman this side of Singapore, but I won't settle for less." *And he adds,* "How different from the pains of youth. Here is no thought of pressed flowers, moonlit walks along the beach. Here is the meaning of the body's work, its need; the rest is wasted time." *That's where I am.*

When I see a beautiful face, an elegant aristocratic face, limpid eyes, delicate exquisite mouth, instantly I see that mouth sucking cock, my cock. Those virgin lips open, open wide, take in the engorged member, hold it hungrily, lasciviously, suck on it, while the cock plunges deeper and deeper into the slender, swanlike throat. And while the dreamlike face is thus engaged, anchored on my prong— no, not anchored, transfixed, impaled—the fawnlike eyes roll up to gaze at me gazing down on her. I want to see everything. The more light the better. Mirrors everywhere.

I want to watch, to savor in minute detail, the disappearance of my cock into an orifice, any orifice, mouth, cunt, ass. Doesn't matter. The more the better. One after another in sequence.

Should one live long enough to imagine such things? Should not such a person be put to death for the good of society? Isn't there something apocalyptic in this? Something to destroy the world? Do you feel this way? Would you tell me? Is it perhaps my own death coming closer, closer?

What am I trying to do, anyway? What do I really want with such a girl? I don't want to hurt her, but it's very clear I'm not wanting to love her either. Maybe I want to disappear altogether up her cunt and enter her womb. Is that what I'm after? What makes this hunger so desperate, so anguished, so altogether insatiable?

Do women feel this way? I can't believe it. This must be a malady of men. Old men. Maybe this is the truth of the phrase "dirty old men." It's a paradox: young men are dirty about the genitals, don't wash properly, don't know how, don't care, whereas old men in their private parts are exceptionally clean, odorless. But in their thoughts! That's a different matter. Young men (at least the young men of my day, maybe it's different now) young men think of true love, whereas old men think of whispering obscenities into shell-like virgin ears.

On second thought Camus did live long enough. He knew all this. He was dealing with the same thing, but euphemistically. He dressed it up, bathed it in Proustian nostalgia. That falsifies it. Because it's not elegant or elegiac or wistful. It's primitive and brutish, the spirit fail-

ing, falling back soiled and tattered and dirty, as the old animal sinks back into the earth.

Sometimes I'm filled with horror at what I am becoming, at what I already am. At a movie—one of those leering teasers—I'll hear the laughter of a man behind me. Soft, gutteral, wet. The kind of laughter that revels in baseness, that finds its pleasure in the pulling down of spirit, the lower and the dirtier the better. And in that laughter I see myself. Not that I laugh; I am silent, chilled, appalled. I want to turn around, scowl, disavow any commonality with one so base. But I am there, the same as he, and that laughter draws my portrait as surely as it does his.

Here is a scene from such a movie. A young man appeals to a woman at night through her shuttered window. He has a tremendous and painful erection, wants relief. Inside the room the woman frolics with her lover, both of them naked. The two of them decide to tease the one outside. "Close your eyes," the woman says through the shutter, "and you can kiss my cheek." He closes his eyes, puckers his lips. She opens the shutters, sticks her ass in his face, he kisses, she farts, then slams the shutters closed. General laughter in the theater, roaring belly laughs, men doubling over, slapping their thighs. The offended and now vindictive suitor goes to a smithy, borrows a red-hot poker, starts back. At this point there is scattered laughter, titillated, exultant. The few who laugh know what's coming, are gleeful because they have got it in advance of others. They are celebrating a greater gift for depravity, a superiority in baseness which enables them to be first in the previsioning of something sadistic, degrading.

I know this baseness, have always known it. It is the common coin, the carnality in us all. But once I rose above it, used it as the fuel to power a transcendent soaring. Out of sex I made love, out of flesh I made spirit. "Who knoweth the spirit of man that goeth upward, and the spirit of the beast that goeth downward to the earth?"

What has happened to me? Am I not the same man? Somewhere? In some lost corner of myself? Can you find it? Why cannot the ideals that shaped and guided that soaring lift me now? They seem empty, weightless. The wind of years blows them about. Husks in autumn. I feel deceived. I suspect them of being illusions, of having always been illusions. What I regret now is lost sexual opportunities. Only that. Only that makes my youth seem wasted. As death get closer only carnal pleasure seems real. It's brutish, it's dirty, it guarantees nothing, but it doesn't deceive.

So maybe I should simply accept the portrait of me drawn by the wet laughter in the dark movie house. Maybe that's all there is, all there ever was. Take it or leave it. That or nothing. Maybe I should climb down from my high horse and stop feeling superior, stop being offended, just slap my knee and roar and whoop it up with the rest of the dirty old men.

XIV ⁓

The Edge

GETTING up from the couch, the patient seems haggard, dejected, beaten. He gives me an anguished, beseeching glance, stumbles out of the room, down the stairs.

I wander about, open the French doors to the balcony. The lace curtains glove my face. Rumble of traffic from Bush Street, footsteps on the sidewalk, a scrap of conversation (". . . it rolled under the bed and I never saw it . . . ever again." "Well . . . So there you are.") What was it? A wedding ring? I shake my head to free myself of empty distraction. In the next block someone is whistling. What is it? "Roll Out The Barrel." Out of tune, desultory, listless.

How do I understand this man? What do I really think? How, for that matter, do I understand myself?

The process of writing must draw to itself some of that energy which, when writing is not possible, reverts to its original form. The creative process, that is, appropriates sexual energy, deploys it to higher purpose. Higher? How do I know that? Well, anyway . . . When the validity of the allegedly higher purpose comes to be questioned, the energy falls back into its original state. Lust. And what this lust wants is conquest.

Does that sound right? . . . I think so. For, surely, when a man gets up in the morning and goes out into the world and works hard all day in the service of shared values to which he gives unquestioning allegiance, expending thereby his resources of assertion, problem-solving, creativity—when such a man comes home in the evening to his family, then surely the sexuality which takes place in his bed must lack that frantic hunger, pre-dation, insatiability, that loom so large in my life. Such values are lost to me. I have fallen into nihilism. And nihilism entails narcissism. Inevitably. Indeed, the rela-tion philosophically of nihilism to belief is identical to the relation psychologically of narcissism to caring.

INDIVIDUAL reason, autonomy, authority, however developed and empowered, are no shield against dread. The faster the development of reason the faster the destruction of the old myths, revealing the illusoriness of all ultimate beliefs—behind each, when you scratch the surface, nothing but the face of death. Dread, despair, and anxiety increase, become finally insupportable. We fall back into our private worlds, and in this condition of narcissism there then occurs a tremendous expansion of sexuality: we are trying to make up sexually for what has been lost socially. The sexual drive is freighted disas-trously with the whole meaning of life. Unable to bear such a burden, it breaks down. And it is at exactly this point that there occurs the degradation of love into lust, and the invasion of sexuality by impulses of predation and violation.

THERE'S *something really crazy about men. I mean about sex. They lose all sense of proportion. Can't see it simply as a good thing. They bring it up close, put it right in front of their noses . . . then they can't see anything else, it blots out the world. Women aren't like that. I'm not like that. If he's tired for a few nights, or preoccupied, or worried, whatever, it's no matter to me. What's important is whether he's nice to me. If he notices me, if he talks to me, if he cares—then it doesn't matter if we don't make love for a while. But with him . . . it's—how do you say it?—a federal case. If I'm tired or preoccupied—just let that go on for a few nights—then . . . no matter how nice I am to him in every other way, it's no go. He gets cold, distant, gloomy. Lets me know in every possible way he's hurting. You'd think I'd betrayed him with his best friend. And nothing will help. Nothing but one thing. It makes me so mad. Being nice to him in bed. That's all it takes. Like water on a dying flower. His folded-in petals open up. Right away. The sun comes out. The sky turns blue, meaning comes back into life, his nihilism disappears, he gets ideas for new work, his world view turns around.*

You know what it is? He'd never admit it. May not know it. His desire is a sin. That's what it is. Not sex in general, not desire in other people. His. But he endows me with the authority to absolve him. If I, independently,

*want him to do to me what he already has in mind to do
to me—if I crave it—he regains innocence. In my depravity! Then for a while he is at peace with himself, on good
terms with God. That's why that gratitude after an orgasm.
I have restored him to grace. And that's what makes his
desire so driven and compulsive. If it were just glands and
hormones, it'd be simple. Like in animals. Would come
and go. Would be simply one part of life. It's not like that
for him. The other way round. Glands and hormones have
been drafted by his scheme for salvation. They work over-
time. Day and night. It's not carnal at all but metaphys-
ical. Salvation for a sinner like him is a never-ending task.*

SEEING others in the light only of our own needs, we
encounter but projections. And what should this mean
to us? Should we mourn those lost others whom we let
slip by unseen? Would it have been interesting to know
them? What if one were so well adjusted that he would
project nothing, see each person as he really is, the center of his own interests?

No occasion certainly for such a one to fall in love.
Aloof from that madness, matter-of-fact considerations
would suffice. Does she share my interest in tennis? Will
she advance my career? What about her genes, her dowry,
her family?

Might it not be, indeed, that this is the very essence of
falling in love? that it's always a yearning for union with
a self-representation? that the desiring, cherishing, adoring, the being *in love*, as distinguished from plain loving,
is necessarily a function of the loved one's being invested

with some split-off aspect of self? some fragment that has not been realized, not mastered, not integrated with the rest, but also not given up, held in hiding, perhaps buried, waiting for that special one who can redeem it? Is it not true that falling in love is always a straining toward wholeness, and the belief that with this special other, one can achieve it?

What sort of loving, then, would be possible to a self that is whole? That hypothetical creature! Immune to the common madness, he would form relationships on the basis of rational considerations.

Should one aspire to such a condition?

Well . . . not to worry! All of us are incomplete, forelorn hosts to unachieved, perhaps inconsistent, but yet unabandoned pieces of self.

To care about some thing or some person means to incorporate a representation of that thing or person within one's self. The scope of the self, therefore, depends on the scope of one's caring. Those who are able to care greatly have generous spacious selves, room for many guests. We admire such people exceedingly. To me the world has always seemed too dangerous for close ties or much caring. This has left me envious of more free and generous spirits, and I have noticed in myself at times a tendency to discredit in others a generosity of which I am not myself capable.

To act . . . act in violation of all that one has been. A break. To throw away the past for a veiled future. One comes to an edge, must turn back or must leap. No way of knowing how far to the other side, or if you will make it, or what it will be like if you do. One looks across a void toward a radical discontinuity. And turns back. Or leaps.

I am moving uncertainly toward such a moment. Should I oppose it in principle? What principle? That it's better to stick with known and familiar evils, though they stifle us, than risk those we know not of? That's no doubt the principle I follow. I distrust impulse, delay it, inhibit it, then rationalize the inhibition. But now that life is mostly gone I know I have cheated myself, that it was fear that determined my inhibition, my cramped life, my profession. I have peddled timidity as wisdom. What do I know?

I KNOW nothing. Know only that I live in desperate ignorance, not knowing how to live. Tormented either by guilt for my sins or by regret at missed opportunities for sinning. Or both together. Life is unmanageable, escapes reason.

THE lace curtains stir slightly to and fro, the gray light shimmers, darkens, becomes a fog, a muffled stillness, fills the room like a pool and I hear the stillness behind me, ahead of me . . .